THE DAUGHTER OF THE PIRATE KING

A few murmurs spread through the crew, and I waited for them to die off before continuing.

"You chose this life because you wanted to be free. Now, you have a decision to make. Join me and sail the Red Sea spreading chaos and debauchery. Or walk down that plank and go lick my father's boots while he steals all the gold from your pockets. The gold you have earned with your sweat and blood. So, which one will it be?"

Also by Iren Adams

Chronicles of Yarrowind

The Age of Change

Heroes of Yarrowind

The Magician
The Daughter of the Pirate King

HEROES OF YARROWIND

THE DAUGHTER OF THE PIRATE KING

Iren Adams

This book is a work of fiction. Names, characters, places, and incidents are the product of the author's imagination or are used fictitiously. Any resemblance to actual events, locales, or persons, living or dead, is coincidental.

No part of this publication may be reproduced, stored in a retrieval system, or transmitted, in any form or by any means, without the prior permission in writing from the copyright owner, nor be otherwise circulated in any form of binding or cover other than that in which it is published and without a similar condition including this condition being imposed on the subsequent purchaser.

Contact the author at irenadams.ink

Original text copyright © 2020 Iryna Alyeksyeyenko

All rights reserved.

ISBN: 979-8-6588-3482-5

To those who seek adventures.

I had walked the streets of dozens of different cities. I had been to places some people believe do not exist. But none of them offered me the same serenity the Red Sea does.

Its domain spreads to the horizon and beyond. Its temper challenges the one of Poriva. Endless riches and countless ships sail through it. Some even find their end in the blue depth.

But no matter where I go, no matter how long I stay there... I'll always find my way back to its vast realm.

                Isabella Dromandor, an entry in her journal

CHAPTER 1

SICKNESS

Isabella was looking out of the window onto the city growing below the keep when the door opened. A man in robes of a scribe walked inside, his hands full of a stack of parchments.

"Admiral," the man said, putting down the stacks next to a taller one on the big desk. "You are here earlier than I expected."

"I have some errands to run in Derevan," Isabella said, walking towards the chair. "But it can wait until tomorrow."

"Did you decide to tell your story then?"

"I have some free time on my hands, and this

should be fun."

"I don't think you will have the same opinion once we start," the man said and settled in his chair. He looked at the long list of questions and back at Isabella. "Let's start with your childhood then."

Isabella's smile slipped off her face, and she took a deep breath.

"Is there a problem?" the man asked lifting a brow.

"No, let's do it."

***

I woke up to the shouts in the other room. I sat up and rubbed the last of the sleep from my eyes. The glow from the moons filtered through the thick curtains and filled the room with a silver light.

Snuggles hanging from my hand, I walked closer to the door. A few candles bathed the kitchen with warmth and brightened the faces of Donovan and Ragnol. They stood in the middle of the room each of them at one side of our dining table, arguing about something in harsh whispers.

I leaned closer, snuggling the stuffed tiger in the crook of my arm. My father's voice was now loud enough for me to hear his words.

"I am already breaking my back..."

"I know," my grandfather's tone was low. "But that's not what she needs."

"One week more and I'll have enough money to

pay the priest," my father's voice had dropped to a low murmur.

"Do you really think this is the best solution?"

"It's the only one I have..."

"Yana is spending the whole day in bed already, she doesn't even have enough strength to stand up. Do you want Isabella to grow up without a parent by her side who could explain to her what is happening?"

"This isn't about what I think or want." My father's hands wrapped around the back of the chair in front of him, his knuckles turning white.

"Well, it isn't about only you either," my grandfather had an edge to his voice as he uttered the words.

"I've had enough!" my father said, stumping the chair on the ground. "I'll deal with this... Whatever this is, later."

Donovan walked across the room, opened the door, and slammed it behind his back with enough power to shake the walls. Ragnol sat on the other chair and rubbed his chin.

Snuggles hanging down from my hand, I walked into the room and approached my grandfather.

"Hey," he said, his lips splitting in a smile and creasing his face in a tender look. "What are you doing up? Did we wake you?"

I didn't answer and climbed into the chair my father had stumped on the ground, not a minute ago.

"Do you want some breakfast?" he asked, giving up on the previous question, and I nodded.

I put my tiger in the chair next to me, where my

mother used to sit when she could still walk. In a few minutes, Ragnol put a plate in front of me filled with pancakes covered in syrup. We didn't have enough money to buy any berries or fruit for it, but it was my favorite dish all the same.

I picked the fork but inspected the food with narrowed eyes.

"Is there some bad news, pop?" I asked.

"Why do you think I have to tell you something?"

"I never get to eat pancakes, only on special occasions, or when you have to say sad things. Like when you had to tell me that momma was sick."

"I taught you too well," my grandfather said, shaking his head.

He pushed away from the counter and settled on a chair next to me.

"As you said, we have talked about Aliyana being sick..."

I frowned. My grandfather had copied the habit of my father calling my mother Yana. If he had used her full name, this must be very serious.

"Well," he said scratching the back of his head. "Your mother is much sicker than we thought. Your father is doing everything he can to help her, but I fear it won't be enough."

I played with the food on my plate with the fork in my hand.

"Don't you want to ask anything?"

"Do I have to?"

"Isa..."

"What?" I asked, lifting my gaze from the plate.

"This must be confusing..."

"I know momma is sick, and I'm aware she isn't getting better," I said with a shrug. "Her skin is grey now, and sometimes she has trouble breathing. And if you are telling me that my father can't do anything about it..."

My grandfather lowered his gaze, brushing some invisible crumbs from the table.

"Is she going to die?" I asked, my voice breaking twice.

My grandfather didn't answer, but he didn't have to. When he failed to meet my gaze, I knew I was right.

"I want you to know that no matter what happens, we all love you," my grandfather said with a frown on his face.

When our gazes met, a smile showed on his lips but didn't reach his eyes. I shrugged, my gaze back on the plate in front of me.

We didn't talk after that and spent the rest of the day alone in the kitchen. Ragnol went to bring some food to my mother, but I knew she wouldn't eat it. She hadn't done so in more than a week. Her bones were now showing from under her skin, but everything she had eaten, she ended up throwing up.

The next day, my grandfather had started teaching me a new language. He wanted to take my mind off things, and I had already heard all of his stories. Some of them more than once.

I had learned the language the people who lived across the Red Sea spoke, but what he taught me was so different. Keromun was what he called it, and it sounded alien when he uttered the words. I wasn't even sure I could shape my mouth and my tongue to pronounce all the inflections he used.

As he taught me new words, I struggled to write them down fast enough before Ragnol switched to another subject. Going from one thing to another, I didn't even notice as the sun crossed the sky.

When my grandfather stopped talking, I lifted my gaze from my notes. My mother had walked into the room, leaning on one of the cupboards. Her face was ashen, her hands trembling. Before she fell, Ragnol slipped a hand around her waist and guided her to a chair, picking my tiger and moving it to the counter.

"I can still walk..."

"I know, Yana," my grandfather said, but didn't lift his hands until my mother was settled in the chair.

"Do you want anything to eat?"

"What will you be dining?"

"The soup is almost ready, but I can make you something else you if want."

"The soup will be nice. I don't want to be a bother."

"You are never a bother."

My mother smiled and turned to me. She leaned closer, a golden locket spilling from under the neck of her gown. She brushed the short fringe of my forehead with her bony fingers.

In Luganda, every man and woman tried to keep their hair short to have as little sins, and bad thoughts pile up and offend The God. The nobles and the priests were the only ones to shave their heads, the only ones who had that right.

My grandfather had come to Luganda from the shores of the Allied Kingdom that lay across the Red Sea. And even though in our house we worshiped the gods of old, the ones that were imprisoned in the Halls of Obliteration for three ages now, my grandfather wanted me to blend with the people around me. We had had enough trouble with my mother's sickness.

"What have you been up to, Isa?"

I looked down at the table and shrugged.

"Don't you want to tell your mother about the things you learned today?" my grandfather asked.

"It's alright," my mother said with a small smile and coughed a few times.

Ragnol passed her a filled to the brim glass of water, but she only sipped on it. Not long after that, he put a plate in front of each of us, and I was more grateful for the food than ever before. At least it allowed me to escape the uncomfortable conversation.

"Thank you, Ragnol. You were always so good to me," she said, before having another fit of coughing.

"Don't talk like this," my grandfather muttered.

My gaze was still set on the table, boring a hole in it. Ragnol and Yana kept the conversation going, interrupted from time to time by a cough from my mother. I wanted to finish the food in my dish and escape the room. Before this could happen, my father walked into the kitchen.

"What in the world..."

"Donovan, my love," my mother said, a tender smile spreading on her face. "Come join us. Your father has made the best soup I have ever tasted."

I shuffled in my seat, but I knew I couldn't escape the family dinner now. My father sat down, his brows met in a single line over his eyes that didn't leave my mother's face.

"Tell me about your day," my mother said.

"How... I..."

"That's a first. You never were at a loss of words in my presence."

"I am just happy to see you here. We haven't had dinner together for a long time," he said and planted a kiss on the fingers of her hand.

My mother smiled and coughed again. This time, she couldn't stop. Her hand came from her lips bloodied. When she managed to take a few breaths in between the coughs, she was wheezing.

"Yana, let's get you to bed," my grandfather said.

My mother nodded, before having another coughing fit. She didn't fight Ragnol as he guided her back into the room as when he helped her to get into the chair.

"Can I go to bed too?" I asked.

My father shrugged, his gaze lost in the space in front of him. He set his elbows on the table and brushed his long raven hair back. I slid out of the chair and picked Snuggles from the counter before slipping out of the kitchen.

I climbed into the bed and covered myself up to

my head with the thick blanket. The sleep took its time to find me. The stars had dotted the black sky and my grandfather's snoring filled the room we shared before my eyelids dropped and the dragons of old danced in my mind.

***

"What did your father do to earn enough money to feed all of you?" the man asked.

"Donovan had mostly worked for Teyo in the Singing Buccaneer. It was the inn close to our house. He also had contacts in the royal guards and did some odd jobs for them now and again."

"What do you mean by odd jobs?"

"Well, the guards have many resources. Some of them get lost once in a while. There is a whole market for that, and my father would find the buyer for any of the goods that had to disappear."

The man shook his head.

"Are you surprised that my father never was honest in anything he did?"

"Not at all," the man said with a small shrug.

CHAPTER 2

DEATH

"Let's talk some more about your mother."

"What do you want to know?" Isabella asked.

"I heard she had lived in the palace before marrying Donovan."

Isabella laughed. "I don't know where you get your information, but I'd love meeting those sources."

"Is it wrong then?"

"Aliyana Dromandor was a noble, but she wasn't related to the Empress in any way. And only she and her family live there. Even the servants and the slaves live outside of its sacred grounds."

"Alright," the man said, writing down Isabella's

every word. "Let's continue then."

***

I woke up before the sun had shown up from behind the horizon. Even my father hadn't woken up, but something was wrong, and I could feel it in my bones.

My tiger nestled in the crook of my arm, I slipped out of the room. I walked into the kitchen trying to figure out what had woken me up. Nothing was out of the ordinary until my gaze settled on the door to my mother's room.

I crossed the kitchen, avoiding the creaking boards on each side of the table, and leaned on the door. Besides the rough surface of the wood, I couldn't feel or hear anything else. The door squeaked as I opened it and tiptoed inside.

My mother lay on her bed. The blanket covered half of her right leg and fell to the floor. Even on such a cold night, she hadn't pulled it tight around her. She didn't stir as I moved closer; her opened eyes fixed the ceiling.

"Momma," I whispered.

She didn't answer, nor moved. My fingers brushed her stone-cold skin as I pulled at her hand. My mother offered no resistance, and her arm fell to the side of the bed. Her head turned and a trickle of blood flowed from her opened lips and stained the pillow.

Tears welled in my eyes, as I stumbled back and fell to the floor. I covered my mouth, muffling a scream, and pushed myself across the room with my feet. As my back met the wall behind it, I shuffled to my feet and darted out of the room.

I crossed the kitchen in the other direction, not caring for the creaking boards anymore. Drying another tear that slipped from my eye, I pushed the door opened and stumbled into the bedroom.

I nudged my grandfather, but it took me more than a few tries to wake him up. He batted his eyelids a few times before understanding what had awakened him.

"What is it, cinnamon?" he croaked.

"Momma is dead," I said.

I tried to clutch Snuggles closer to my heart, but I must have forgotten it in my mother's room.

"What?" my grandfather asked, sitting up and scratching his head.

It had taken him a few seconds before he jumped to his feet and darted out of the room. He was always silent when he walked, to not wake any of my parents. But now, Ragnol banged doors and made a few chairs fall as he rushed across the house.

"By the Gods!" a cry full of angst reached my ears and made me shiver.

In a few moments, my father's loud footsteps came reached my ears as he walked into the kitchen.

"Why all this noise?" he asked and cleared his throat.

I walked closer to the door spying on the

happening through the half-opened door.

"It's Yana..." my grandfather answered dragging his feet as he walked out of her room.

"What do you mean?!"

Donovan didn't expect an answer either. He pushed my grandfather out of the way as he ran into his wife's room. Another earsplitting howl crossed our small house.

I walked out of my room and settled into a chair. My grandfather leaned on a counter, scratching the back of his head, his gaze set on the space in front of him.

My grandfather hadn't moved when my father stumbled out of the room and fell into a chair. His head in his hands, his long raven hair fell over his face between his fingers.

"Isa... We have to talk about what happened."

"Who cares about any of this talk?" Donovan mumbled from under the veil of his hair.

"Donovan, Isa is your daughter! She needs some guidance."

"Yana is my wife!"

"Cinnamon, go to the room, try to sleep some more. We'll talk later, alright?" my grandfather asked with a sad look in his eyes.

I nodded and slipped out of the room.

"You can't talk to her like that. She just lost her mother!" Ragnol said in a hard voice not waiting for the door to close behind my back.

"Hmm," my father muttered again.

"She's too little to understand what is going on...

She needs us to help her through this."

"By the Gods, will you stop with your lectures?! My wife is... dead."

I didn't stay to listen to the rest of it. Sliding the window open, I slipped out of the room and on the deserted streets of Query.

A cold breeze ran through my hair. My head cleared, the wind taking the last of the sleep with it. I brushed the remaining of my tears from my eyes and wrapped a scarf around my face.

I started walking with no clear destination in my mind. My only desire was to get away, as far away as possible.

A few slaves and servants crossed Query on some business for their nobles. Other than that, only some beggars sat on the corners. Their skin hung loosely over their bones as they stretched their arms towards me. But I steered clear of their bony fingers.

I wandered through the city until it woke. When the streets started to get crowded, I found an unoccupied bench in one of the parks.

The shadow of the wide leafed trees allowed the air to stay refreshing during the day, and I welcomed the breeze that ran through my short hair and cooled my head.

My eyes watered as the thought of my mother no longer being alive crossed my mind. Since she fell sick, we stopped playing together, and with time some days when she would be too weak to get out of bed, I wouldn't even see her.

I brushed the tears out of the corners of my eyes

again, pretending it was the sun that blinded me before anyone could notice my outburst. A bench creaked, and I saw a boy with a shaved head slip in the seat next to me. A tunic of bright green brushed his skin with the morning breeze. He leaned with his back over the bench, but his gaze darted around and over every person that walked through the park.

"What do you want?" I asked.

The boy shrugged. "Felt like you needed some company."

I didn't answer, the only thing present on my mind was my mother's glassy eyes as her head turned to me.

"Don't you have something else to do? Hundreds of slaves to bother?" I asked.

The boy chuckled, not bothered by my remark in any way.

"Why would you refuse a friendship?" he asked in a light tone.

I looked at him, but besides his wicked smile and his piercing brown eyes, his features had nothing remarkable.

"What is your name?" I asked.

"Koen, yours?"

"Isabella."

The boy smiled and stretched his hand.

"Nice to meet you, Isabella."

I shook his hand with a small frown. For a noble to talk with someone from my origins wasn't a common thing. With my ear-long hair and my light brown skin, I would be a black sheep among the nobility.

"What happened to you?" the boy asked. Without a doubt, he must have noticed my red eyes.

"My mother just died."

"My condolences," Koen said.

I nodded and offered him a small smile.

"Where do you live?" the boy asked.

I knew he was trying to take my mind off things too hard to deal with, and I was grateful for that.

Afraid to disrespect the belief that strong emotions offended The God the people worshiped in this land. I had been trying to hide my tears for the past few hours.

The only safe place to show my emotions, cry, or scream would be at home, but I didn't feel like coming back yet.

"Close to the port," I finally said. "Early in the morning, when the sun starts to show behind the horizon, there is this small breeze that carries the smell of the sea into my bedroom."

The boy nodded, taking in each of my words, his gaze no longer darted over the people around us but has settled on me.

"I suppose I don't have to ask the same question of you. You must be living in the palace or at one of the noble houses," I said pointing at his tunic.

"No. These were a gift. Actually, I am the son of one of the priests. I live in the Highest Temple."

"Oh... All this small talk must bore you then."

"I like to hear what others have to say. I find it fascinating how people slip so much information without noticing. Sometimes it comes in handy."

"What did you learn from what I said?" I asked arching a brow.

"I can tell which house you live in."

"How is that possible? I only gave you a few details!"

"That's all I need. You said you could smell the salt in the air when the morning breeze entered your room."

"So?"

"If you would live in the houses around the Singing Buccaneer, you would have your windows shut during the night. Because if not, you would hear the drunken sailors chant as they left the tavern. Their singing can wake up even the dead."

"Yes, but that leaves a whole district."

Koen nodded, "But the first few lines of buildings next to the port are warehouses and shops. No one lives in them. And to the west, your house would be too close to the sewers, the morning breeze would only bring the smell of human waste into your room."

Koen seemed to think for a moment before adding, "Your house must be the one with the light atop the blue door."

I shook my head, but a smile had shown on my face. Koen was smart, maybe even sharp enough for us to become friends.

The bells of the Highest Temple took me out of my thoughts. I had to get back to our house.

"I have to be back to the temple," Koen said. "Morning prayer is about to start, and we have a silent agreement with my father that I have to honor."

"I have to get going too."

Koen smiled and stretched his hand. I did the same, and he clapped my palm twice.

"Until the next one, Isabella."

I nodded, and the boy took off into the city and in a moment disappeared in a crowd of people. I stood up and went back to our home, with the blue door at its entrance.

***

"What's on your mind?" the man asked when Isabella stopped talking.

"He doesn't talk this much, nowadays."

"I am surprised to hear he ever did," the man said checking his notes.

"You will never know everything about us. No matter how much time you spend questioning each one of us about our lives."

"Well, nothing will ever stop me from trying," the man said with a small smile.

CHAPTER 3

DEPARTURE

"While we are on the subject," the man said, picking a fresh parchment. "There is not much information about Donovan from before his days as the Pirate King."

"I would assume he doesn't like talking about it."

"And why would that be?"

"No matter who his subjects are, a king can never show any weakness," Isabella said and bit her lip.

***

My grandfather had found someone to take care

of my mother's body. Embalmed and dressed, she lay in her bed. Her finest gown spread around her in a halo. Blue in color, it was one of the few possessions she kept after leaving her noble house to marry my father.

Teyo and some other men my father knew from the Singing Buccaneer came by our house the next day. They picked Yana's body and carried her to a small temple set in our district. The priest was already waiting for us in his crimson robes.

My grandfather and my father shared the faith in the Gods of Old, the same belief they had transferred to me. But my mother stayed faithful to her religion even when she had followed my father away from the life of riches and comfort.

In her past life, the ceremony would happen in the Highest Temple with the High Priest leading it. Thousands of people would attend the ceremony. Even the empress might have graced my mother's memory with her presence.

Instead, the three of us stood in an empty temple. The paint scolded off next to the ceiling, and the dust hasn't been brushed from the corners for a long while.

The only other people present were the men who had carried my mother into the temple and a priest in patched and faded robes.

I don't remember what the priest had said before they cremated my mother's body. But I'm sure it was as good composed as the temple was well-kept. My whole attention was captured by Yana's face. After the embalming, her skin had lost its pallor and added brilliance to her chestnut hair. Even with her bones sticking out, my mother had regained some of the beauty she had lost during the last month of her sickness.

The acrid smell of the burning flesh hit my nose as the priest had set the pyre on fire. The smoke lifted and went out through a giant chimney carved in the roof, guiding the spirit of my mother into the land of her God. Tears slid down my cheeks and a sob escaped my lips, but no one had said anything. My grandfather stretched a hand with a handkerchief in it, tears welling in his own eyes.

My father's gaze was set on his wife's body devoured by the fire. Even when it became ashes, he hadn't moved. He didn't budge even when the priest had collected her ashes and carried her remains into the Hall of the Dead. My grandfather sighed and guided me into the streets, leaving my father alone in the temple. Neither one of us said anything as we walked the crowded streets home.

The sun had hidden behind the horizon when Donovan stumbled through the door. As we ate dinner, the only thing that broke the silence was the clanking of the silverware on the plates. My grandfather stared at Donovan with narrowed eyed as he swayed in his chair, spilling the stew over the polished table.

As soon as my father had finished his dish, he stood up and wobbled to the counter. He took a bottle of strong spirit and filled a glass to the brim with it. He downed it all in one sitting and filled it again. My grandfather observed the scene but didn't say anything.

The next days were a monotonous passage of time. My father stayed at home, spending his days with a bottle of a strong spirit as a company. My grandfather kept teaching me Keromun and told me the stories about the people who spoke it.

"What is the use in it?" my father slurred after a few days of silence.

"Your daughter has to learn," my grandfather answered in a dry voice.

"Why? You taught me the same things, but what did it bring me? Huh?"

My grandfather narrowed his eyes.

"What? Are you going to spur some more wisdom on me now?" my father said. He drained another glass and ran his long fingers through his greasy hair.

"Go to your room, Isa," my grandfather said.

I never argued when my grandfather asked me that, and that day wouldn't be the day I started to do so. I wasn't very interested in what they had to say to each other, and picking up my notebook, I slipped out of my chair and into my room.

As soon as the door closed, the shouting began. I climbed into the bed, covering my head with the pillow and my blanket on top.

I didn't notice as I fell asleep, but I woke up to some noise in the kitchen. My grandfather's snoring stopped. Something else dropped to the ground, and Ragnol cleared his throat and rolled to the other side.

I sat up and rubbed my eyes. My grandfather

might know what was happening, but I wanted to investigate. Picking Snuggles in my arm, I walked into the kitchen.

My father stood in front of one of the cabinets. He picked one of the jars with dried dates and a pouch with walnuts that my grandfather had stacked on the shelf, not a day ago. Donovan stuffed his leather backpack with all the items he had gathered and tied a knot on top.

"Dad?" I mumbled.

My father stopped what he was doing and turned on his heels.

"Isa? Why are you out of the bed?"

"What are you doing?" I asked, ignoring his question.

My father sighed and walked closer, guiding me to one of the chairs. He sat on the one next to it and cleared his throat.

"My father wanted to avoid this," he said running his hand through his hair. "But I don't think you are too young to understand."

I frowned and looked up to him. He brushed my fringe out of my face and smiled.

"I'm doing this for you and my father."

"What do you mean?"

"What happened to your mother, should have never come to pass. I want a comfortable life for you two."

"But you can stay and do it from here..."

"No, cinnamon, I can't. I had an offer from a friend of mine. I have to go."

I shook my head, tears welling in my eyes.

"I don't want you to leave..." I whispered, my voice breaking.

"The decision has been made. A lot of people are counting on me."

"But... That's unfair," I mumbled.

"Life rarely is. But you will learn it yourself, one day."

Donovan disheveled my hair and offered me another crooked smile. He snuffed the candle, picked his bag, and walked out of the kitchen.

I stayed for a long while in the darkness and emptiness he had created. Tears slid down my cheeks, and I brushed them away with my sleeve, the fabric becoming drenched.

The breeze entered the room again, making the curtains dance and bringing the smell of salt. I shivered and dried my tears for what I told myself was the last time. I slid out of the chair and walked into the room my mother had taken as soon as she got ill. My grandfather had changed the sheets, but it still smelled like her.

I snuggled into the bed and took a deep breath. I filled my lungs with her scent, trying to catch every last bit of it. A little smile on my face, I fell asleep.

My grandfather found me in the morning, a sad look in his eyes.

"Hey, cinnamon. Do you want some pancakes?"

I nodded, and he picked me in his hands as he carried me into the kitchen. I noticed he had put Snuggles away. I had left it on the table when I went to spend the night in my mother's room. I didn't say anything because I didn't want to see it again.

My grandfather slid the plate filled with pancakes in front of me, the thick syrup falling over and drenching the dough.

We ate in silence, no one uttering a word about my father's absence of my father or the fact that I had taken my mother's room. We didn't have to do it. My grandfather always told me to make my own decisions, but be ready to live with the consequences. And I was finally ready to grow up.

***

"My grandfather used to tell me that Donovan left because I reminded him too much of Aliyana," Isabella said, playing with one of the trinkets around her neck.

The locket was made of gold and glistened as she moved it between her fingers.

"But you don't think so?"

Isabella took a deep breath.

"No matter what I think... The truth of the matter is that he ran away from our home, and he never stopped running."

CHAPTER 4

MAGIC IN THE AIR

The man walked across the room and brought a glass of water to Isabella.

"Thank you," she said and dipped her lips in the cold liquid.

The man picked a new parchment and studied it over the rim of his glasses.

"When we talked the last time," the man said lifting his head from the parchments. "You said that your family came from the Allied Kingdoms."

"Well, now it's called that. When my grandfather lived here, it was a bunch of duchies scattered around."

"I know that," the man said with a smile.

"Then what's your question?"

"How did he manage to befriend the elv[es?]"

"From what he told me," Isabella said, [leaning] back in the chair. "The elves used to come to Logena to trade. But they didn't need anything, their craftsmen able to do wonders of their own. Townsfolk resented them, found it unfair. Except for my grandfather who would welcome them in his house."

"Why is that?"

"I never asked him that... He was interested in their culture, I guess. But it certainly helped him. They shared some of their lore with him and taught him the Lost Tongue. Well... Bits and pieces they knew. The rest he learned from the desert wanderers."

"How did he meet them?"

"I'm not sure, but I did see them once."

"I'm all ears," the man said picking up his quill and laying a new parchment in front of him.

***

The house had become much smaller in the turns that followed my father's departure. Donovan hasn't come back since the day he left seven turns ago. He was doing well, or so my Ragnol told me. He did send us money, but my grandfather never talked about what Donovan was doing. Ragnol had trouble finding things with which to occupy me. I spoke the Lost Tongue now as fluently as my grandfather did, and there were no longer any new stories he could tell me. He had told me about the artifacts of the elves and made me memorize the maps of Luganda without any explanation. But even his vast knowledge no longer offered me new distractions. So, I got used to slipping out of the house at every opportunity. I ran through the streets, climbed the roofs, and observed the people that crossed the city on the endless errands.

The loneliness had been my constant companion. Other kids my age were either working to help their parents feed their households, or came from the noble family and didn't even spare with a glance.

On one of such days, I was coming back home from my escapade. My hair plastered to my skin with sweat, my lungs burning with heat, I ran across the roofs.

I stopped in my tracks when I noticed a family on the street below me. A woman held a young girl in her hands as her husband picked sacks filled with their belongings and carried them inside.

A young man my age stood some distance away, kicking a loose stone around.

"Either help or go somewhere else before you get in trouble," the woman said, turning to her son as he kicked another stone and it ricocheted from her leg.

The boy muttered an apology and dashed around the corner before his mother could change her mind. Unable to take my gaze of someone my age running through Query, I followed him across the maze of streets hiding in the shadows of the roofs. He stopped a few times to look around. His eyes even climbed up to the roof once, but I hid behind a column and away from his gaze.

With a shrug the boy would dash again through the narrow streets and around the corners, coming closer to the Seventh Garden. In a sunburned city stuck between the inhospitable desert and wide sea, Luganda's first Empress Enriqua had built a marvel. Flowers of each color and variety blossomed next to fountains with carved statues. Wide-leafed palms hid the tender bushes and bulbs from the burning sun during the day and offered an oasis for those who sought some reprieve from the heat and sand.

The boy stopped next to a field of irises forming a pattern with different colors bright even at the late hour of the night. I crept as close as I thought was wise. The boy leaned to breathe in the scent of the flowers before picking one of the black irises in his hand. The light from the moons spilled over the patterns of ink dancing on the skin on his arms under the rolled up sleeves, and I gasped.

"You shouldn't be afraid of me," he said into the empty space before turning his head to where I stood hidden behind a palm. When I didn't answer he added, "I know you are there."

I muttered a curse and stepped forward. The boy had a crooked smile on his lips as he stepped closer. I squared my shoulders, but a blush crept up my cheeks.

"Who are you?"

I didn't answer, not ready to give my name to a stranger.

"As fast as a thief," he started circling me. My gaze traced the boy's path around me, but I kept my ground. "As proud as a noble..."

I didn't answer, waiting for him to give away more about himself than I would share about myself. His gaze ran over my lodged between my teeth lip and back to my eyes.

"You tell me your name, I'll tell you mine."

"Isabella," I said before I could stop myself.

"Nice to meet you, my lady," he said curtsying in front of me, a mocking smile on his lips. "My name is Brook."

I tried to stiffen the giggle building up in my throat as the boy changed from menacing to funny.

"And what brings you to this part of Luganda?"

"Strictly pleasure," he answered, stepping closer. The flower twirled in his hand, one way and then another.

I fought the urge to step away, my breath caught in my throat. Before I could decide whether to run or break the small barrier of space between us, Brook brushed a few grains of sand stuck to my cheek. He tucked the flower behind my ear, his fingers tracing the long black locks of my hair. My skin tingled where he had touched it, and a pleasant feeling purred in my chest.

"You might be born in this land, but I've never seen someone as beautiful as you are."

The giggle finally broke out from my lips and echoed through the empty garden.

"You have what, fifteen-sixteen turns behind your

back?"

"So?"

"You'll talk about undying love next when we've just met?"

"So pragmatic for someone so young."

I snorted but couldn't bring myself to look away.

"You won't believe me then?" he asked.

"No, I'm not that naive."

Brook leaned forward, his breath tangible on my skin. His lips trailed mine, before plating a deep kiss. I pushed myself away. Deep down in my heart, I regretted my action. I wanted to stay close to him. I shook my head trying to force the thoughts out of my mind.

"I have to get going."

Brook picked my chin between his fingers, forcing me to look him in the eyes.

"I'll be waiting for you, iris. And when we meet again, you better believe me."

I shook my head and pushed away from his too comforting touch. I ran the streets back home, even the cold night breeze unable to erase the fluster from my cheeks.

I ran past the first window of our house and had to take a few steps.

A group of men sat inside my grandfather's room, each clad in the shadows of a brown toga. Their hoods were down, the scarves lifted from their faces. All men had long hair that trailed behind their shoulders, except for my grandfather and one other man.

His eyes met mine through the glass that separated us into two different worlds. He leaned towards my grandfather, whispered something in his ear, and walked out of the room.

Before I could move, the man opened the door and stepped outside. His pepper and salt hair glistened under one of the moons on the sky.

"And who would you be?" the man asked.

"I'm Isabella Dromandor. What do you want from my grandfather?"

The man chuckled. "He invited us in."

"Why? And who are you?"

"I would rather learn why you are spying on us."

I opened my mouth but closed it again, not understanding why I should tell him my secrets when he wasn't ready to share his.

"Tell you what," he said in his deep voice. "I'll tell you who I am, but you will do me a small favor."

I thought about it for a moment before answering with a nod.

"I'm a magician from over the seas. I was taking refuge with the desert wanderers who seemed to know your grandfather. They told me so many great things about him that I wanted to meet him in person."

"A magician?"

The man opened his hand and fire danced on his palm before disappearing as he rolled it into a fist again. A small smile danced on his lips as I looked him in the eyes.

"Now, the favor you promised."

"But you haven't told me your name!"

"Names are unimportant, and they might change depending on who is calling you."

I frowned trying to understand what he was trying to tell me.

"So, the favor?" he asked.

I nodded. A trade was a trade. Even if I wasn't satisfied with the answers the man had given me, but I knew it was the only thing I would learn.

"I would appreciate you forgot I was ever here. You have too many things to do, too many battles to fight. I wasn't supposed to meet you."

The man offered me his hand, and I slipped it in his. We shook them, and the man was gone.

I looked around, but I couldn't remember what I was doing there. A fog covered the memories of the day. With a yawn, I slipped into my room and fell on my bed.

∗∗∗

"Wait for a second," the man asked, dropping his quill.

"What?" Isabella asked.

"You met this man, and he made you forget he ever walked into your life?"

"An interesting character, don't you think?" Isabella asked.

"But you do remember him now?"

"I don't know what exactly started it. But since the

events in Kholtrem, my memories came back to me... I remember this man, even though I have no idea who it is."

CHAPTER 5
FAMILY REUNION

"Had Donovan ever return home? Or did he stay away?"

"He did," Isabella said with a frown.

"And?"

"What?"

"What did your father say when he showed up? What did he do?"

"I don't know," Isabella said with a shrug. "I didn't stay long enough to chit-chat."

"What do you mean?"

"Well, this is what happened."

***

The smell of pancakes reached my nose, and I rushed out of my room into the kitchen. The memories from the past day were hazy, but I didn't want to delve into what my mind hid from me.

I walked to the table, eying Ragnol from under the curtain of my hair that has grown down to my shoulders.

"I didn't put poison in it," Ragnol said with a chuckle, but I didn't laugh.

"You want to tell me something."

With a loud sigh, my grandfather sat next to me and scratched the back of his balding head.

"We have someone coming to visit us."

"Let me guess," I said, picking up a fork and stuffing my mouth full of pancakes. The syrup sweetened the acid of blackberries and raspberries but didn't help me swallow it. I continued through the thick dough that filled my mouth. "Donovan decided to show up, didn't he?"

"Isa, he is your father."

"He hasn't done much to honor that title."

My grandfather sighed.

"Don't you think that if Donovan wanted to see us, he would have come earlier?" I said, picking another batch of pancakes and drooling them with syrup.

"Well, he will be here tonight," he said.

I smirked, already preparing another of my escapades.

"You will stay here for the reunion over the

dinner," my grandfather added before I could plan too far ahead. "You have to promise me that."

"It's been seven turns. I don't have anything to tell to that man..."

"Cinnamon, please... Do it for me."

"Alright, pop."

My smile was gone, and I stuffed my mouth with more pancakes, chugging the cha to wash it down. As soon as my plate was empty, I slid out of my chair and went into my room.

I spent my day with different books until night fell, and I found my way into the kitchen. My grandfather had lit a few candles to chase the darkness away.

"Will he show up, or will he do what he always does?" I asked when Ragnol had turned the heat under the pan filled with water for the cha for the sixth time.

My grandfather leaned on the counter and scratched the back of his head.

"He won't show up, and you know it."

"Isa..."

"What? How long are we supposed to wait for him?

"No more, for I have arrived," a voice came from the entrance.

My father stood next to the door, his skin tanned and creased by the sun, but other than that unchanged.

My breath caught in my throat as Donovan offered me a crooked smile he had on his face when my mother used to be around. His raven hair glistened in the candlelight as he walked closer and leaned to plant a kiss on my forehead. I twisted away, and my grandfather clicked his tongue.

"It's alright," my father said before Ragnol had time to chide me.

"Can I offer you some cha?" my grandfather asked.

"Do you have any coffee? I grew quite used to this bitter drink."

I snorted. My grandfather threw me one of his looks that said I had to cut it. He turned to Donovan and nodded.

"I must have some in the pantry. I'll be back in a minute."

My father dropped on a chair and played with the spoon next to his cup.

"So," he said, sitting up and clearing his throat. "How has it been?"

I crossed my arms over my chest and turned my head away.

"Isa... Come on, talk to me," my father said, leaning closer.

"You want to talk?" I asked, turning to look him straight in the eyes. "Remember when you left, and I begged you to stay and talk to me and be there?"

"Isa..." My father winced and downed his gaze. His voice came out in a whisper.

"Remember how I cried, and you said to me 'Life isn't fair.'? Well, tough luck."

"Isa, listen..." my father started again.

But my grandfather had walked back into the room, a jar filled to its half with the dark and bitter powder.

"How are the two of you doing?" Ragnol asked.

"Just fine," I said, standing up. "Guess it's time for the two of you to catch up."

"You promised."

"I guess no one in this family can follow through with those."

"Isa..." my grandfather started again.

"And while you two are at it, you should stop calling me that. Never liked it, never will!"

Before any of them could react, I ran out and slammed the door behind my back. I wove away from the port and deeper into the city.

I only stopped when I was out of breath. I leaned over my knees as my throat burned while getting more air into my desperate lungs.

"Being a while since I've seen you," I heard a familiar voice.

I lifted my head to see a young boy next to me, but I couldn't tell who it was. Until I noticed the brown eyes that darted over the street around us and back to me.

"Koen," I said, lifting my hand.

He clapped mine twice and smiled.

"I would love to stay and catch up," he said, his gaze shot to the street next to us. "But let's say, I have a meeting that I want to avoid."

He had turned away when I caught the hem of his shirt.

"Mind if I come?"

He looked at me for a second, but then his gaze slid over my shoulder into the street.

"As long as you can keep up the pace," Koen said.

He didn't wait for my answer as he spun on his heels and ran in the opposite direction he was going. I rushed behind him, trying to catch up. His retreating back disappeared behind corners before reappearing at the end of the street. The streets were dark, the honest folk had already closed their shutters, the candlelight spilling from the inside of their windows.

***

"You ran away?"

"You know me," Isabella said, crossing her arms.

"Yes, that's why I am surprised." The man shook his head. "You were always cool-headed when making decisions. So, why this?"

"I was resentful of what happened when my mother died," Isabella said and bit her lip. "I still am."

"And Koen?"

"What about him?"

"What did he have to say about it?"

Isabella shifted in her chair, before clearing her throat.

***

The roofs passed under our feet as we ran across

them and jumped between the edges, as we crossed Query and put as much distance as we could with the things we wanted to stay away. Our pursuers had lost us even before we climbed the buildings, but Koen hadn't stopped. Our pace had slowed, but he still led us closer to the heart of the city.

We stopped when the silence reigned around us, the shadows chased away by the warm candlelight spreading from inside the Highest Temple. I dropped at the edge of the roof, my legs swinging over the void, formed by the five-story building. My gaze wandered over the temple in front of me with its wide arches and high domes. Koen sat next to me, his breathing as shallow as mine.

"You can run, girl." Koen chuckled and dried the sweat rolling down his brow.

"Will you tell me what was chasing us?" I asked pulling my wet hair away from my face.

Koen hesitated for a second, but then took a heavy leather pouch out from the folds of his toga and passed it to me. The contents clinked on the roof next to me, and a gasp escaped my lips.

A few dozen golds lay next to a glistering black jewel bigger than any coin around it. I lifted my gaze to Koen's who observed me with narrowed eyes.

"If you ever rat me to the guards, I will cut your throat in your sleep," he said and pursed his lips. "And no one will ever know it was me."

I burst into laughter, my shoulders quaking.

"I am not joking."

"I know, my fellow priest," I said unable to

contain the laughter. "But let me tell you two things. First, that is not how you make friends, and second, you wouldn't be able to do it even if you tried."

Koen didn't take his gaze off me, and I offered him another wide smile.

"Wait here," Koen said, jumping to his feet.

He picked one of the coins and jumped over the cornice. My eyes wide, I leaned over. Koen had a wild grin on his face, hanging from the ledge of the balcony. Letting go of it, he grabbed another one below and followed his descent.

I leaned back on the roof, making a pillow with my hands. The stars shone above me in different patterns. I could make out the seven stars of the Crow and the Dragon next to it. I drew lines with my finger over the Large Spoon and the Northern Spear. Vega, the brightest star on the sky set at the point of the shining spear twinkled over the dark canvas. Before I finished naming all the stars and constellations, Koen had climbed back and settled next to me.

"What are we looking at?" he asked, gazing at the sky above.

"Have you ever wondered if it's true? The stories behind all these constellations."

"You mean like the Azure Feather that was supposed to be dropped from the crown of Enriqua, the first Empress that ever reigned in Luganda?"

I nodded, and Koen shrugged.

"That's not very priest-like of you," I said, sitting up.

I didn't add anything else. The blood rushed to my

head and made the black dots spread in front of my eyes.

"Well, cutting pouches of imminent nobles who are too busy kissing the boots of my father to see their riches stolen, isn't very priest-like of me either. But I am not a priest, after all," he said.

I snorted. Koen smiled and passed me a small bundle wrapped in a waxed paper with greasy spots all over it.

The smell of spices hit my nose as I unwrapped the offering. Between two thick slices of bread, lay a dripping piece of meat garnished with vegetables and a large ration of sauces.

Koen had his mouth full as he bit into the sandwich. His gaze wandered over the temple, the tiled rooftops, and the flowering balconies. One of his feet dangled over a neck-breaking fall he had jumped into without a second thought.

We ate in silence, enjoying the meal under the shining stars. Koen rolled his waxed paper in a ball, picking the bits stuck between his teeth with a nail of his little finger.

"When will you tell me why you ran away this time?" he asked, not turning his head.

I sighed and folded my wrapping in half, flattening the bend before doing it again.

"I am not in a mood of talking about it."

"What if I offered you this?" he asked, picking the jewel from the pile and passing it to me.

"Are you trying to buy my answer?" I asked with laughter on my lips.

"All information has its price..."

"That bauble must be expensive."

"I want to know the answer, and I am willing to pay whatever the price you set."

He stared into my eyes, unflinching. I picked the stone from his opened palm and lay back again. The blackness of the jewel was only pierced by the bright stars behind it.

"My father came back for a visit," I said.

"How long has he been away?"

"Seven turns now... He left not long after my mother's death."

Koen didn't answer, as he lay next to me again.

"I don't know why Donovan thinks he can show up after so much time. And he expects I'll give him love when he'd never given me any? He hasn't sent a single letter to me..."

"I heard some rumors in the temple the other day."

"What about?" I asked playing with the stone.

"A man who is sinking empire's ships as if they were made of paper. He has managed to organize the pirates in a powerful fleet. Well, not as powerful as the empire's one... But the empress is scared of him. The nobles in the temples can't stop whispering about it.

"He calls himself the Pirate King, but I heard a noble utter a different name. Donovan the Eagle."

I propped myself on an elbow and stared at Koen.

"Tell me," he said, turning his head to me. "Do you know many men in this land called Donovan?"

"I have to go," I said, standing up and brushing

the sand that had sprinkled my grey skirt.

Koen sat up, looping one of his arms over his folded leg. I stretched my arm, palm up, and offered his jewel back to him.

"Keep it," he said with a shrug. "A deal is a deal."

I frowned but put the jewel in a pocket hidden in the folds of my skirt.

"We will see each other soon, daughter of the Pirate King."

I shook my head and climbed the building down. I rushed across the deserted city back to our house and stumbled through the unlocked door. My grandfather was the only one inside, a candle melting away on the table in front of him.

"Young lady," he said, standing up. "This behavior isn't acceptable from someone risen in this house."

I snorted, and my grandfather frowned.

"Oh, you are serious, aren't you?"

"Of course, Isa."

"While my father... Wait, no. While *your* son does what he is doing in the Red Sea... I think I can have some leeway in what I am and what I am not allowed to do in this house."

"Isa..." my grandfather said, his voice earning an edge to it.

"And I remember telling you this already. My name is Isabella. It isn't much of an effort to add a few more syllables, is it?"

Before Ragnol could answer, I spun on my heels and left the kitchen with a loud bang of the door of my room. My grandfather didn't follow me inside. He never did. I don't know if it was to respect my privacy, or because the memory of Yana was too painful for him to ever set his feet in this room.

I walked to the desk I had in the corner and pulled the middle drawer. Lifting the false bottom, I took the golden locket out of it. My finger ran over its rim, and the memories of my mother flooded my mind. Not the way she was when she was sick, but when I was little and she would play with me. I would grab the locket, and my mother would laugh trying to free it from my chubby fingers.

Before the bad memories came again, I put the locket back in place and slipped the black gem next to it. Sliding the drawer in place, I buried myself in the folds of my blanket and fell asleep.

***

"Koen was already a thief at that age?"

Isabella chuckled, "You'd better ask when there was a time when he wasn't one."

"You talked about priesthood?"

"His father is the High Priest on the Highest Temple. He thought his son would follow his steps, but Koen had found something much more to his liking."

The man leaned back in his chair, a deep frown on his face. But then he picked up his quill again and added a few more lines to his parchment.

CHAPTER 6

A FRIEND IN THE SHADOWS

Isabella shook her head and put a wild lock behind her ear.

"Why are you so interested in Koen?" Isabella asked when the man didn't lift his gaze from his notes.

The man lifted his head and smiled.

"I hadn't had an opportunity to learn much about him while you described your adventures at Kholtrem," the man said. "And yet, he is not a simple thief..."

"What do you want to know?" Isabella asked, hey eyes regaining a twinkle that was gone before.

"When was the next time you met with him?"

"Two turns later, actually..."

"What happened?"

"I was in need of some information," Isabella said with a chuckle. "And Koen is the best man for it."

***

I sat on the roof I've last seen Koen. My skin itched from the heat and sand under the folds of the scarf wrapped around my head and face and the shirt on my body.

"You are in my spot," Koen said from behind my back, and a smile spread on my face.

I clapped his hand twice before unfastening my scarf.

"It's been a while," he said, sitting next to me.

"I see you took a few steps further away from the priesthood," I said pointing at his grey toga. But even if its color has changed, his head stayed shaved.

"Some steps are worth taking if the result brings enough profit. Fewer people notice my passing," he said with a smile. "If the need arises... I haven't thrown the white one yet."

No matter his change in clothing, his features stayed the same. His brown eyes had already studied the place around us, evaluating the surroundings and pinpointing an escape route.

"What do you need?" he asked.

I passed him a pouch. He unfastened the knot and

took the black jewel out of it. His gaze darted to me.

"This was a payment, why do you return it?"

"Because I need some information, and you are the best thief in town I know."

"The only thief you know."

I chuckled, "Maybe... Will you give it to me?"

Koen thought about it for a while, turning the stone between his fingers.

"If I have it or if I can find it, it will be yours."

He pocketed the stone, and I smiled.

"What will it be then?"

"Donovan."

"Ah, yes. I should have guessed. What about him?"

"What has happened to him since the last time we talked? And when is he coming to Query?"

Koen sighed.

"What is it?"

"There is some unrest in the sea lately. The Pirate King is no longer such a revered title. He has built himself a throne, but he holds his place with an iron fist."

"Someone must be endorsing him if he still reigns over them."

"That's true, sister," Koen said with a smile. "He has struck a deal with someone in the empire's fleet. They help him stay where he is, in return, none of the pirates attack the fleet ships."

"That's an interesting deal to make... For someone who calls himself the Liberator."

"Exactly what I thought. But everyone is afraid of

him. No sailor will speak ill of him. That is they want to keep sailing the Red Sea and not swim with the fishes."

The wind had thrown my long curls over my face. Koen smiled and passed me a red bandanna.

"And here I thought you were a devoted follower."

"Am I in trouble, priest?"

Koen laughed while I wrapped the bandanna over my hair.

"So what about his next landing in Query?"

"This one is trickier. He hasn't come here for a while. Not since his last visit. I'd guess he doesn't feel welcome here."

My feet dangled over the cornice, my gaze wandering over the city, the next question forming in my head.

"What would it take for him to come?"

Koen looked at me with a lifted brow.

"You know the deal," I said with a shrug.

"Yeah, who doesn't have any issues with their parents," he said with a chuckle. "Anyway, from what I gather, there is a commemorative date coming. If he would come, it would be for this."

I bit my lip full in thought.

"What's your plan?"

"What are you going to pay for this information?"

"I might have told you too many of my secrets," he said, another chuckle escaping his lips. "Well, let me buy one of those sandwiches, and we can discuss the details."

I pretended to think about it for a second before answering with a nod.

"You've got yourself a deal."

He wrapped a scarf around his head and climbed the wall down. I observed him blend with the crowd and look over the wares of one stall and another.

A blade of a knife flickered under the sunlight. One of the merchants had no longer his pouch. A moment later, the coin from the pouch was exchanged for the sandwiches in the merchant's shop.

"Does it count as payment, if you got it for free?" I asked trying to stifle the laughter when Koen had climbed the building.

"The price is always subjective, my friend," Koen said and passed me the sandwich. "It could be a result of the whole livelihood for one, but only a grain of sand for another one."

"And that's why you will be always setting the price."

Koen shrugged and bit into the sandwich.

"What are you going to do when Donovan comes?" he asked between two mouthfuls.

"I'll ask him to take me with him," I answered trying not to stain my clothes with the trickle of hot sauce.

Koen snorted, but in a second was coughing, the crumbles stuck somewhere in his windpipe. I struck his back and a few times, and he nodded, drying the tears from his eyes.

"Tell me you have something else up your sleeve," he said when he could force some air into his lungs again.

"Improvisation is my strength," I answered, taking the last bite. "Did these get smaller, or did we got bigger?"

"Don't change the subject."

I sighed, rolling the wax paper in a ball.

"I can't stand this place anymore. I love my grandfather, but his stories about great adventures... Let's just say they make me want to get out there and write my own future."

Koen smirked and picked some of the food stuck between his teeth with the nail of his little finger.

"Don't dare laugh at me."

"I'm not, but if you will have any need in my services... I will be around."

"Wreaking havoc no doubt!"

"I prefer shadows and silence."

"I have to go. Thanks for this," I said lifting my hand with the rolled wax paper in it.

"Anytime."

Koen nodded and offered me his opened palm. We clapped twice, and I was gone, tracing my way home.

***

"Koen was very eager to help."

Isabella nodded. The man didn't ask any other question staring Isabella in her eyes.

"What?"

"Was there any romantic interest from his part?"

Isabella's laughter resonated through the room. The man didn't say anything else waiting for the answer.

"Do you see what I meant when I said this would be fun?"

"I don't quite understand."

"Not all the troubles that raged between the priest and his son were are a complete mystery to me."

The scribe waited for Isabella to make her point.

"Even though he enjoyed and loved women, Koen preferred men as a company."

The man lifted a brow. "Isn't it forbidden in Luganda?"

"Yes, it is. His father still thinks he will be devoured by ravens of death one day. And he doesn't forget to mention it each time their paths cross."

CHAPTER 7
THE PLAN

"Alright, let's go back to Donovan. Did he show up?"

"He loved my mother. She meant more than the whole world to him," Isabella answered her gaze lost on the space ahead of her.

"But you weren't sure if he would accept your demand."

"He had loved Yana. I'm not so sure about his love for Ragnol or me..."

"Tell me what happened," the man said dripping his quill into the pot of ink.

***

I walked into the kitchen where my grandfather was arranging some breakfast for us.

"You are up early," he said with his back to me. "I thought you would drag your ass here at noon again."

I yawned but didn't answer as I took a seat at the table and slumped on my hand. My grandfather kept to the steaming pot in front of him, paying no attention to me.

I was still yawning and rubbing the sleep away from my eyes when Ragnol put a dish in front of me. I picked a spoon and drew circles in the spiced pumpkin porridge.

"If you insist on letting your hair long, at least tie it up before you'll have more porridge in your hair than your mouth."

I sighed but unwrapped the red bandanna from my wrist and tied my curls up with it.

"After your last night escapade, I thought you would be hungrier than that."

I looked up from my plate and gulped.

"Don't look at me like that, girl," he said with laughter on his lips. "You thought you fooled me, didn't you?"

"I..."

"I won't tell you what to do, you are no longer a child," he said, putting another spoonful of porridge in his mouth. "Even though it was your habit when you were one."

"I had to get out there, explore the world you tell me so much about... And then I made a friend."

"You don't have to tell me everything. It's your life to live."

We ate in silence, and the food managed to wake me up.

"I thought we could have a small dinner tonight. You and me... It has been a while," Ragnol said after finishing the last of his cha. "Your mother would be celebrating her fortieth birthday today..."

"Sure," I said with a small smile. "Do you know if Donovan will come?"

"I hadn't had any news since... Well, since the last time he came." Ragnol shrugged before adding, "But who knows, cinnamon? Maybe he'll come."

I sighed and helped him clean the table. We spent the day each with our own things. As the night fell, we lit some candles and set the table for three as we had done this night since the day my mother had died. But we no longer waited for Donovan to show and filled our plates with roasted beef and baked potatoes. The beef melted on my tongue, and the potatoes burned my mouth.

A knock came, and both of us looked at the door. I dropped my fork, and Ragnol wiped his mouth with the napkin. After a sigh and a walk across the room, he opened the door.

On the other side, Donovan stood, his raven hair shining under the glow of the stars in the sky and the light over the door.

"Father," he said with a nod.

He walked past Ragnol and across the kitchen, the heels of his boots clanking on the wood flooring laid in geometrical patterns.

"I see you didn't even wait for me," he said breaking the silence.

My grandfather slipped in his seat, and Donovan followed. I opened my mouth, a retort ready to slip. I thought against it as Ragnol looked at me with narrowed eyes before turning away.

"You changed so much, Isabella," my father said leaning in his chair towards me. He picked one of the potato wedges with his hands and slipped it in his mouth, before licking his fingers.

"In this house, we use cutlery to eat, or did you forget that too?" Ragnol said with narrowed eyes.

"Always such a stickler to the rules," Donovan said with a chuckle.

He put some of the potatoes and beef on his plate but picked a bowie knife from his belt to cut his food.

"Won't you ask me how my life is going? What is that I do?"

"I know what you've been up to."

Ragnol ate his food, not sparing a glance in Donovan's directions. I shuffled in the seat and drank some of the water from my glass.

No one uttered a word as the dinner went on. When we finished the meal, my grandfather cleaned the corners of his mouth again and leaned back in his chair and cleared his throat.

"For how long will you be staying in Query?" he asked.

"A week, maybe less. I'm still deciding on..."

"And then what?" Ragnol asked interrupting him.

Donovan shrugged. "I'll go back to what I was doing."

I swallowed and bit my lip. It was now or never.

"Can I come with you?" I blurted.

The sound of clanking silverware as it fell on the table followed my question. Both men turned to me wide-eyed.

"I would love to, but..." Donovan was the first one to regain his composure.

"The life he's leading is not for you," Ragnol said, staring my father down. "Go to your room. We will talk in the morning."

Donovan looked between the two of us.

"Pop, you know I am bored in here," I said, standing my ground.

"Don't argue me on this!"

"I..."

"Isabella, I agree with my father," Donovan finally said. "You can't come."

I squared my shoulders and held my head high, "Fine."

But instead of going to my room, I walked to the entrance door. The shouting started a moment after I had banged the door shut behind my back. I leaned on it for a second, before shaking my head. I pulled the scarf tight around my face and crossed the empty streets on my way to a familiar place.

***

Isabella shook her head, and the man stopped writing.

"What's on your mind?"

"That was some wishful thinking..."

"What do you mean?"

"Donovan does what he wants, disregarding whatever anyone else asks of him."

"Why did you do it then?"

"I guess I wanted to see if there was some love in his heart for me..."

The man nodded but didn't write anything down. "Where did you go?"

Isabella bared her teeth in a smile. "I went to see a friend."

***

I paced from one side of the roof to the other as if performing a silent ritual. An invocation of a thread of hope that I could pull and the solution would uncoil in front of me.

Before the priest finished with the evening prayer and the bells struck again, a figure slipped in the shadows of the roof. He walked closer before untying his own scarf and revealing a half-smile.

"To what do I owe this pleasure," Koen said after we had clapped our hands in the welcoming gesture.

"Donovan is here," I said, not stopping my pacing.

"So I've heard."

"He won't take me with him."

"Hm," he said leaning on the roof of the neighboring house, crossing his arms on his torso.

I stopped pacing and squared my shoulders.

"What?" he asked.

"You said you would help!"

"I did, and I will..." he said with a shrug. "But first I need to know what is that you want to do."

I sighed and dropped in a cross-legged seat.

"I could sneak on his ship and hide," I said after a while. "Donovan wouldn't throw me into the sea, would he?"

"I wouldn't make any bets on that..." Koen said with a shrug. "You'll have to come up with something better than this."

I chewed on my lip.

"Come on, spit it out. I can see it on your face that you've come up with something."

"I will steal his ship," I said with a wicked smile.

"And what can I do for you, captain?"

I laughed, but Koen's didn't, a spark I've never seen dancing in his eyes. He pushed away from the wall and stepped closer. I had to fight the feeling in my gut that screamed to step away or run.

"If you want to be a captain, better start acting like one!"

"But..."

"Donovan hadn't climbed to his seat of power with weakness and hesitation! Even if you don't have a plan, even if you don't know what to do next... If you want to command the Golden Eagle's crew, you have to conquer them with your grit."

I frowned and bit my lip.

"What will it be then?" Koen asked again, stepping closer, searching my eyes for an answer. "Will you live in the Pirate's King shadow your whole life or will you carve your own future?"

I nodded and took a deep breath. I already knew I needed from Koen.

"Go to the port. Donovan's crew must be at some tavern down there, spending money on cheap ale and willing women. I have to know what they think of their captain. Meanwhile, I'll go pack and pretend everything is as it should be. We'll meet tomorrow here at the same time."

Koen nodded and in a flash was gone.

The next day, I waited for noon, so I could get out of my room and eat my breakfast as if nothing was brewing in my head. I didn't have to pretend very hard as Donovan had captured all my grandfather's attention.

They bickered with each other about everything and anything. Even the color of my father's shoes didn't seem to please Ragnol. When the evening came, we had another silent meal. My grandfather kept to his plate, throwing an occasional glance at my father with his narrowed eyes. Donovan in his turn offered me one apologetic smile after another.

I struggled with my impatience and forced myself to eat my stew one spoonful at a time. The silent treatment was getting boring, and my leg jumped up and down under the table. As soon as I finished my meal, I stood up, put my dish on the counter, and walked to the door.

"Where are you going?" my father asked, turning in his chair.

"Out."

"Aren't you too young to be running the streets of this city at this late hour of the day?"

"And why do you think you have any say in it?"

My grandfather sighed. "Donovan, let her go."

"She's just a child!"

"You couldn't wait to talk about me as if I wasn't here until I actually left, huh?" I threw at my father before planting a kiss on my grandfather's head. "Later, pop."

My father growled, but I slipped out of the house before another argument erupted.

The streets were as calm as the previous night, but I hadn't stopped to witness the beauty of the city plunging into darkness and the thousands of lights spreading through it. I climbed the roofs earlier than we agreed, but a cloaked figure was already there, observing the city below its feet.

"Koen," I said, offering my hand.

He clapped it twice before turning his gaze back on the temple in front of him. A priest shuffled up the stairs one at a time, leaning on an ornate staff.

"What are we looking at?"

"The old man loves his theatrics." Koen shook his head.

"Wait, your father is the High Priest?" I asked with wide eyes.

Koen answered with a shrug, his gaze glued on the temple even if his father was gone.

"Anyway," I said shaking my head. "What did you learn?"

Koen turned to me.

"Aren is your man."

I lifted a brow. "My man?"

"The strongest man on board of the Golden Eagle, he might also be the smartest right after Donovan. But the Pirate King keeps him as a cook, so he couldn't start any trouble.

"Except Aren loathes his captain and has been recruiting other sailors on his side. The mutiny is imminent. Donovan might even know about it, but he must be thinking he has enough time to deal with it. That's where you come in."

"Why would the man follow someone else if he already wants to stage a mutiny?"

"Aren has numbers, but many sailors are still loyal to Donovan. A mutiny will force a slaughter. Aren wants to avoid that."

"A pirate with a soft heart?"

"Some of those who oppose Aren are Donovan's friends or are too afraid of him. But if his daughter comes and says that she is there to guide them on the right course, most of them will follow, even Aren."

I chewed on my lip, thinking it over.

"Aren will be waiting for you tomorrow at nightfall in the Singing Buccaneer."

I looked at Koen, with a frown on my face. "What did you do?"

Koen smiled, the spark from the previous night back in his eyes. "Tomorrow is the best day to do it. Your father will be thinking that all is well and his sailors are drinking in the inns across the harbor while his daughter is on another of her nightly escapades. He wouldn't suspect his ship is gone. A day or a few later, when he will finally notice that you are gone, it will be too late for him to catch you right away. Giving you enough time to slip away."

"Alright," I said. "How will I recognize him?"

"I will be there," Koen said.

I nodded and lay back. After a moment, Koen lay next to me.

"Do you think it will work?" I asked turning my head to him.

"It will. But it's not about what I think. It's about what I know."

I rolled my head back and gazed at the stars dotting the sky above.

***

"I see no obstacles can stop you..."

"I had help," Isabella said with a shrug. "But it's better to search for solutions rather than cry in defeat."

"Weren't you afraid of what you were about to do?"

"I was. Scared to my bones. But I couldn't show it."

"Why is that?"

"Koen was right. To be able to sail the Red Sea on the Golden Eagle required courage. If not, the sea would swallow me whole and spit me out broken."

CHAPTER 8

THE GOLDEN EAGLE

"Did your grandfather have any idea of what you were about to do?" the man asked.

A perfect smile stayed on Isabella's lips, but a glint of sadness spread in her eyes.

"He was a smart man."

"I have no doubt he was... But that doesn't answer my question."

Isabella shrugged. "I'm not sure I have an answer to that. He never said anything..."

***

My grandfather put a hand on my arm as I dropped the dishes on the counter.

"You are not going out tonight?"

"I wanted to rest a little," I said with a shrug.

Ragnol scratched the back of his head and sighed. "Well, I'll leave you a pouch with some nuts and a couple of sandwiches if you do decide to go out later tonight."

"Pop..." my heart tugged in my chest, and I had to swallow a ball growing in my throat.

"What? Can't the old man show his sensitive side every now and then?" he said and opened his arms for a hug.

I leaned in, and he wrapped his arms around me.

"Try to stay safe, will you?" he said pulling away.

He picked a rag, rubbed some soap in it, and started cleaning the dishes.

"Go," he said when I hadn't moved. "Get some of that rest you were talking about."

I shuffled into my room, doubting my decision. But then I remembered all the stories he had told me over the turns and all the things I wanted to do. I walked to my desk in the shadows of Laraith.

Pulling the middle drawer with the false bottom, I emptied my hidden stash on my desk making as little noise as possible. The little treasure I've been collecting for turns glistened under the moonlight.

A few dozen coins of different value lay next to a golden locket that I slipped around my neck and my leather-bound journal that I failed to keep on a regular basis.

Everything packed in a cotton shoulder bag, I lay in my bed and stared at the ceiling, waiting for the house to settle. My father and my grandfather had argued for an hour as they always did since Donovan had showed at our door, but I tuned them out as I did when I was but a child.

As soon as both men went to their respective rooms, and our house plunged into silence, I slipped out into the kitchen. As promised a heavy pouch was waiting for me on the counter. I put in in my bag and gave the kitchen one last look. A sparkle caught my eye, and I walked closer to the table. A leather belt lay on the table, a pair of pistols with golden engraving holstered inside. My finger ran over the patterns of cold metal and sharp jewels. With a smile plastered on my face, I picked the holster and wrapped it around my waist.

Koen was waiting for me in the alley next to my house and joined my side, neither of us stopping. He had donned wide pants and a loose shirt, passing as any other sailor in the city. He had even found a knitted round cap that hid the absence of hair on his head.

"I see you managed to lay hands on some beautiful weaponry."

"Are you accusing me of thievery?" I asked him with a lifted brow.

"Me? Never!"

I chuckled, but it was a burst of nervous laughter. The thing I was about to do was more terrifying than

I was willing to admit.

We reached the Singing Buccaneer in less time than I had hoped for, but then again my home was two streets away. Koen opened the door for me and let me inside.

A few men lifted their gazes from the filled tankards in front of them, but others kept their attention on their drinks or the cards and knuckles that they were playing. Koen weaved his way through the crowd to a man at the back. An untouched tankard of ale sat at the table in front of him, even though from his relaxed composure it was obvious he has been in here for a while.

Koen dropped on the bench in front of him, and the man nodded before turning his gaze on me. I followed Koen's lead and slid on the bench next to him.

"What can I do for you?" the man asked, twisting his tankard in his hand.

Koen leaned on the wall, his shoulders relaxed. His features showed disinterest, but his eyes ran over the crowd searching for any trouble.

"I think we could be of help to each other," I said.

The man's gaze slid down my figure, hovering over my waist where the stolen pistols hung in their holster.

"And what could that help be?" he asked bringing the tankard to his lips. As he lowered it, the quantity of the ale hasn't changed.

"I heard you're in search of some support."

"And what's that to you?"

"As the daughter of the infamous Donovan the Eagle, I could help with the loyalty of your crew. In exchange, you would teach me anything I don't yet know."

"A woman in sea... Some of the men might think it would bring bad luck."

I licked my lips and threw a glance at Koen. He didn't react, his gaze still lost on the crowd that filled the room.

"Then I would dissuade them of thinking of me as anything else but their captain."

A small smile broke on Aren's face.

"Alright," he said. "When do you want to do it?"

"Tonight."

Aren's eyes widened, and a cough escaped his lips.

"There is no point in waiting," I said squaring my shoulders. "Unless you want to wait for Donovan to figure out what you and some of your followers are brewing."

Aren nodded and gestured for a young blond-haired man who sat at another table to come closer. I hadn't noticed him, but the absence of interest in Koen's gaze told me he had acknowledged his presence and found nothing of danger.

"Gather the crew," Aren said. "We are leaving in a few hours. Any man who won't be on the ship when we pull the anchor can forget his pay."

The boy nodded with such enthusiasm that he had to straighten his loosely tied bandanna. In a second, he was tapping some men on the shoulders and whispering something in their ears. The men nodded and wrapped up their games, finished their drinks, and gathered their companions.

"Follow me," Aren said standing up.

We exited the bar, weaving the deserted streets closer to the port and towering ships harbored in it. The smell of salt in the air made my heart beat faster in my chest.

One of the ships caught my eye. Its boards painted black, the ship would be invisible in the darkness of night. An eagle of gold sat on the front ready to take flight, its wings spread wide.

We walked the plank to the deck, a few men already on board, preparing the ship for the departure. An hour passed and more men came on board. Some threw a glance in my directions but followed with their route as soon as they caught Aren's gaze.

As the last of the men boarded the ship, I looked at the sky. The three moons were full that night, distanced by the stars but brighter than any of them.

"Are you coming?" Aren asked and took me out of my observations, but he wasn't talking to me.

Koen shook his head.

"We will be leaving in less than an hour," Aren said. "Say your goodbyes and leave before we ease the sheets. That is if you don't want to swim back to port."

With another nod in my direction, Aren left to oversee the last preparations. Koen walked to the railing, and I followed suit. My gaze ran over the city that spread in front of me.

"This is it then."

"I think this is far from over," Koen said with a shrug.

I chuckled. Koen looked up at me and smiled. He offered me his hand, and I clapped it twice. Without adding anything else, Koen went down the gangplank and disappeared from view.

"Hey, Aren!" a sailor with a nasty scar running down his chin shouted from the other side of the ship. "Where is the captain? Or are we sailing out without him?"

The men stopped what they were doing. Some walked closer to Aren, others formed a guard behind the owner of the scar. Donovan's most loyal dogs were eager to stir some trouble.

As he turned to me, Aren had a muscle jumping up and down his jaw. "This is your cue."

I dropped my bag and walked towards the man. My boots echoed through each corner of the ship, my hand searched for a reassuring touch of the pistol on my belt.

"What's your name?" I asked.

"Kal is what the boys call me," he said in a smug voice. "What's it up to you, girl?"

"Well, Kal," I said. "I am Isabella, daughter of Donovan the Eagle. This ship is now mine, and I am your new captain."

Kal laughed, and a few men behind him joined. I threw a glance around. Those who stood next to Aren had their hands on the weapons on their belts. But some part of the crew was observing the scene, not ready to join one side or the other.

I took the pistol out with a silent prayer on my lips that Donovan had loaded it. I cocked the hammer and pointed it at Kal's groin. The laughter ceased, and the man tried to wiggle free.

"Listen here, you little shit. I said I'm your captain now," I spat as I pressed even harder, and the man cried out. "You either take your head out of your ass and say 'Aye, captain' each time I give you an order, or you will be food for fishes."

The silence on the ship was deafening. No one moved, not even to take a breath. I stepped closer, close enough to smell the ale on his breath.

"Now, which will it be?"

"Donovan will not like this..."

Before Kal could finish what he was saying I pulled the trigger. A howl broke through the port, resonating in the silence. Kal fell to his knees, blood seeping through his fingers on the deck of the ship. Some of his supporters leaned to help Kal, but I pulled the other pistol out and cocked the hammer.

"Did I say you could move?!"

The men moved back leaving Kal slosh around in his own blood.

"You harlot! You will pay for this!" Kal spat through his clenched teeth between pained whines.

I laughed.

"Threats of a dying man, that's a first..." I turned to the other men on board. "This is not the best entrance, I agree."

No one dared to speak up, waiting for me to finish what I had to say.

"But... Let me say one thing. I know you all have been tired of the tyranny my father has imposed on you when he had promised you freedom and riches!"

A few murmurs spread through the crew, and I waited for them to die off before continuing.

"You chose this life because you wanted to be free. Now, you have a decision to make. Join me and sail the Red Sea spreading chaos and debauchery. Or walk down that plank and go lick my father's boots while he steals all the gold from your pockets. The gold you have earned with your sweat and blood. So, which one will it be?"

All the men turned their eyes down as our gazes crossed.

"Well, then," I said. "I believe it's time for you to start moving your asses. We had left half an hour ago! Aren, put Kal in the brig and have someone clean all this blood."

"Right away, captain!" Aren said with a smirk on his lips. "You heard her boys. Move before you get one more bullet under your skin!"

The crew moved as one and in a few minutes, the Golden Eagle glided away from the port and into the Red Sea. Soon, Query was just a speckle of light on the sky filled with stars.

***

The man leaned back in his chair and brushed his quill with his long fingers. "You stepped into your role pretty quickly."

"It had to be done, or I would be the one on the deck, bleeding to death."

"But you had to kill someone for that. You had no trouble with that?"

"If you are asking me whether I regret it... Then the answer is no, I don't. But I remember what I had done, and Kesareth will judge me for my sins when my day will come."

CHAPTER 9

THE DOGS OF THE PIRATE KING

"How was the pirate life? Did you find it to your liking?" the man asked picking a new parchment.

"It wasn't easy. But I never felt better than when I was sailing the Red Sea from one end to the other."

"And the crew?"

"I won them over, with time."

***

I stood at the wheel, the sun high in the sky. The deep blue sea spread around me in every direction, hiding fishes and lost ships below its darkness. Grey clouds gathered to the east on the spotless sky. A storm was coming.

Aren walked to my side.

"Spit it out," I said as the moments passed and Aren hadn't uttered a single word.

"What's the plan here?" he finally said.

"What do you mean?"

"We have been sailing the Red Sea for three turns now. We have seen the Allied Kingdom; we have raided dozens of ships..."

"It's what I promised."

"I know." Aren nodded, his gaze lost on the clouds in the sky.

"So, what's your point?"

"Don't take it the wrong way... We had filled our hold with chests full of gold. But some men wonder what the goal is."

I let my gaze wander across the horizon as I mulled his words over.

"Who is against me?"

Aren smiled. "A few old comrades of Kal's have been spreading gossip."

The wind blew some of my hair across my face. As I moved it away, the first droplets touched my skin.

"What could calm them down?"

"Action is good, but sometimes they need to spend their money on some ale and women to make them remember why they love the sea."

"We've been in different ports."

"A few hours to resupply don't count, captain."

"I'll think about it."

Aren didn't move, something else bothering him.

"Also," Aren said, a muscle jumping up and down his jaw. "Some of the men still question your authority."

"Ship ahead!" a cry came from the crow's nest.

"This conversation will have to wait," I said to Aren before turning to the lookout. "What colors?!"

"Red and black!"

"That's a first," Aren muttered.

"Let them sail close," I said to Aren. "But tell the boys to get ready for trouble. This can go either way."

Aren nodded and started shouting orders to the men. The beauty of organized chaos unfolded in front of me. The sailors rushed across the ship, checking their weapons and taking positions. The scene marveled me as it always did, and I wondered why any of them would want to go back to a port.

"Heath!" I shouted.

A young man of roughly my age appeared at my side. A leather cord held his wheat-blond hair behind his back, and a cleanly shaved face offered me a nod.

"Captain?"

"Take the wheel," I said stepping away. "And keep your eyes. Anything happens to her, and it is on your head."

Heath nodded and took my place as I moved to the left side of the ship and picked the spyglass from my belt.

The ship was closer now, no longer a simple black point on the horizon. But even so, it was still much smaller than the Golden Eagle. Few of the ships that sailed through the Red Sea could tower over the Golden Eagle, and they belonged to the empress's fleet. Neither one of them would be able to overtake us. We had to trim the sails to let the other ship catch up with us.

As its dirty sails grew against the blue of the sky, I counted the men on board. A shine from one of the men told me their captain was doing the same.

"I see twenty men," I said putting the spyglass down. "But there will be more."

"They won't attack first," Aren said. "They want to parley."

I nodded but checked if my pistols were loaded. The ship sailed closer, its board next to ours. I stepped on the rail, holding on to one of the ropes.

"I know the ship, but who is this girl in front of me?" the man with a tricorn hat said.

The rain was leaving dark stains on his faded red shirt that battered his body with the strong wind that had lifted.

"Interesting situation," I said. "For I don't know who you are either."

"My name is irrelevant, but I might guess yours. Isabella, is it?"

"Wouldn't it be fair for me to know yours then?"

"Captain Dacian," he said and a smile spread on the man's face.

"What brings you to this part of the sea, Dacian?"

The man scowled at my disregard of his title but squared his shoulders. "A large bounty is set by the Pirate King, and I think I will be cashing it in."

"What is that he seeks?" I asked with a lifted brow.

The captain laughed, and all the men on his ship followed suit. On the Golden Eagle, the silence reigned. No one in my crew had drawn a weapon only because neither Aren nor I had given the order. As their fingers twitched, I knew their hands itched for the comforting touch of the steel.

"Oh, Isabella," the man said shaking his head, the mirth still audible in his voice. "He wants his ship back and the crew dead."

His hand went for his pistol, but I was faster. Both of my barrels were pointing at his chest, the hammers cocked.

"Don't do anything stupid, Dacian," I said. "Do you want to visit the halls of Kesareth so soon?"

"You and your pagan gods," Dacian spat.

He never finished drawing his pistol. Two dark stains spread on his shirt, and the captain fell back. My crew moved as one, drawing weapons and discharging them on the sailors of the other ship.

I heard a thump of a body at my side but didn't turn around. I drew a saber from my hip and jumped across the gap between the two ships. A sword came slashing down at me. A clank of steel and Aren had deflected the blow. With another swing, the sailor fell to the deck clutching his crimson-stained shirt.

I ducked as another blade came hurtling at me. I

threw a dagger retrieved from my boot. The man took it out of his bleeding throat, but it fell through his fingers. He dropped on the deck, a puddle forming around him. I picked my dagger up and slashed at another man's belly as he rushed across the deck with a sword high above his head.

"Knobhead..." I muttered.

I threw a look around and saw my crew cornering the last couple of men who had any fight left in them. The rain battered down on the ship, cleaning the blood from the deck.

"Please... please," a voice begged from under my feet.

I crouched trying to see through the lattice. A few hands reached for me through the holes in the wood. I jumped back and cried out.

"What is it?" Aren asked.

I didn't answer as I rushed across the deck and climbed the steps down. A large lock hung on the door.

"Give me your pistol," I said, not looking to see if Aren had followed.

The cold metal touched my skin as he slipped his weapon into my hand. I cocked the hammer and shot at the lock. After the smoke had cleared, I tugged at the metal, and it crumbled in parts in my hands.

The door had been shut tight, and I leaned on it with my shoulder before it gave in. The stench hit me right away. I coughed in my elbow and slipped my bandanna over my mouth.

"By The God..." Aren muttered at my side.

I walked inside. The figures around me dashed to the sides with a rattle of chains. Their clothes had stains on them of different colors and ages. Their bodies frail, the older ones hid the smaller ones behind them. As my eyes ran over their faces, it hit me. The cry for help was in the language they used in the Allied Kingdom.

"That piece of garbage," I muttered. "He was a slave trader."

Aren pulled me by my arm until I faced him.

"You know full well; the slaves are a normal thing in Luganda."

"Yes, but..."

"This is reality. Think carefully about what you do next," Aren said with a wince.

A few men from my crew had slipped down the stairs and into the room. Some were looking at the scene in front of them from the corridor. Others were still on the deck but could hear everything through the lattice. He didn't have to tell me my men paid attention to every word I said.

I shook Aren's hand off my shoulder. "This might be a normal thing in Luganda, but we are not in her majesty's domain. This is the Red Sea, and we all fight for our freedom in its vast arena!"

The sailors from my crew didn't utter a word, their gazes glued to my figure.

"Donovan the Corrupt and his bunch of ill-mannered nitwits will not set the standards by which we live our lives! And we certainly won't trade human life for profit!"

The men whistled and clapped their hands. I looked back at Aren. He was clapping, a smile on his face.

"Now, sorry bunch of chowderheads! Do I have to spell it out for you? Free these people and take anything of use from this ship!"

A clamor of voices deafened me. The men moved to break the chains, helped the confused men and women up to their feet, and guided them to the deck.

"Captain, what of the prisoners?" one of the sailors from my crew asked.

"Tie them to the mast. They deserve to suffer the same fate their ship will."

I climbed the stairs back up where my crew was passing barrels and bundles to the Golden Eagle. A few of the men helped the former slaves across the gangplank that covered the gap between two ships rocking on the waves. The rain battered the wood and soaked my clothes in a few moments.

Aren walked to my side from the depth of the hold, brushed the water from his brow, and clicked his tongue.

"What?" I asked with a roll of my eyes.

"We should be more cautious from now on," Aren said.

"We shouldn't be discussing it out in the open then."

The sailors parted as we moved to the Golden Eagle and across the deck.

"As soon as the cargo is loaded, blow her up!" I barked at my men. "Heath, set course to Luganda. We are going home, boys!"

The sailors cheered and picked up their speed with the promise of a trip to the safe port.

Inside my cabin, the mood wasn't as cheerful as I set a glass of rum in front of Aren and poured one for myself. I settled into the chair and kicked my feet on the table.

"I found this," Aren said and put a leather-bound parchment on the desk atop the spread sea charts and some of my journals.

I set the glass down and picked the parchment.

To anyone who encounters the Golden Eagle out in the Red Sea,

Consider the ship lost in battle, its captain, a renegade of our cause. Its reclamation is not a priority, but if possible would be rewarded.

All the traitors who turned their backs on our nation should be eliminated.

The Pirate King

I cursed and threw the parchment back on the table.

"Donovan has set a black mark on each one of us," Aren said swirling the rum in his glass. "Even you..."

"I see," I said swallowing my own share and refilling it again.

"But... There is an upside."

I lifted my gaze to Aren's.

"You can forget the worries I expressed earlier.

The men will stand by your side after what happened. You showed them who the captain is here, and what are our values."

"Well, all this might have solved some of the problems, but added a lot more to the heap."

"The problem was already there, we just didn't know about it," Aren said with a shrug.

I stood up and walked to the dusty window at the back, my hands clasped behind my back.

"We keep sailing the sea, do what we always did."

Aren was silent as I turned back to him.

"That's what you wanted to hear, isn't it?"

"Yes, and that we have to find some allies."

I smiled as I turned back to him.

"I know just the man who will be able to help us with that."

***

The man had a wild grin on his lips when Isabella stopped talking. "A pirate with values..."

"I thought there would be no judgment here."

"This was just an observation."

Isabella crossed one leg over the other. "What did you want me to do? Bring them to Luganda and sell them into a life of misery and suffering?"

"It might have brought you a profit."

Isabella didn't answer, her arms crossed over her chest.

"What happened to them?" the man asked

checking something on his parchment.

"Most of them joined the crew," Isabella said. "But we brought back anyone who wanted to return to the Allied Kingdom on our next trip."

CHAPTER 10

HOME

"Who was the man who would be able to help you?"

"Koen, of course," Isabella said with a shrug.

"A thief would solve all your problems?"

"A thief of secrets, a collector of contacts, a keeper of information."

***

I paced the deck from one side to the other as the coast grew on the horizon. As soon as the warships came in the view in front of us, I stopped and bit my lip.

I haven't visited Query for more than five turns, and I haven't seen my grandfather or had any news from him in all this time.

We sailed between two warships guided by a ship pilot, but I knew that Aren or Heath could land the Golden Eagle without any help or guidance.

"Listen up!" I cried as the gangplank dropped down from the ship to the harbor. "We'll be here for at least a week. But be ready to be back on board as soon as the order reaches you!"

"Aye, captain!" the sailors cried in chorus.

I turned towards Aren who stood by my side. "Keep an eye on them, will you?"

"Aye, captain. If you need anything I will be at the Singing Buccaneer," he said before following the sailors.

I stepped down into the port from the ship and walked into a guard waiting next to it.

"Might I see some papers?"

I passed him a leather-bound parchment, and my gaze followed the sailors who walked past the guard and into the city. Aren stopped, but I motioned for him to keep walking.

"You'll have to come with me."

"I don't think so. We both know why you want me to come with you," I said, unhooking a pouch from my belt and passing it to the man. "But I really want to avoid it. This should cover any misunderstanding that might arise with my father."

"He is your father?" the man said, his eyes wide.

"Let's make a deal," I answered, putting a hand on his arm and leaning close. "You make sure you're here each time I come to port and that no one else notices my passing, and a pouch this size will land in your hand."

"What if my captain finds out?"

"Well, that's a risk you have to take."

The man looked at the pouch at his hand and licked his lips. He nodded, and I walked past him into the city.

Indiscreet gazes followed me through the streets and to the house. I took a deep breath and before even more people stopped to look at me, I knocked on the door. My grandfather didn't take long to open it. He looked at me for a long moment before stepping away and letting me in.

"Hey, pop," I muttered, my gaze down.

"Come closer, cinnamon," he said, opening his arms.

His hug felt the same way it did as when I was a child. Warm and welcoming.

"Are you hungry?" he asked.

Before I answered, Ragnol shuffled around the kitchen, taking out dishes and setting the table for the two of us. He put some flatbread on my plate and dropped a pan full of spiced meatballs in the middle of the table.

"Aren't you mad?"

"Even if I was, it's a long time to hold a grudge," he said. "But I always knew you would leave. You weren't one to stay in one place for long."

I crumbled the bread between my fingers.

"How's the sea?"

"Much more exciting than I ever thought it would be," I said a smile spreading on my lips. Ragnol chuckled and shook his head. "But the trouble is always close."

"Your father..."

"Donovan isn't very fond of me right now."

"He was furious when he discovered what you did," Ragnol said another chuckle coming to his lips. "But when he found out, you were already gone... For a few days too. Let me tell you this: I've never managed to make him this mad."

I smiled and picked a meatball with the bread.

"For how long will you be staying?" Ragnol said after a while.

"A week, no more. I am on the run after all."

My grandfather nodded.

"There is someone you should see." I lifted a brow, and my grandfather wiped his mouth with his napkin. "A young man has been circling this house for some time. If I didn't know better I would think that he's marking the house for a sweep."

I bit my lip to stiffen the laughter. "I'll deal with him. But now I want to spend some time with you."

Ragnol smiled and asked about my adventures. I talked for hours now the protagonist of my own tales. My grandfather followed every one of my words and chuckled each time I told him about the troubles I would get myself into. When I got tired of talking,

Ragnol took the lead and told me about the changes in Query that happened in the last five turns.

"Go," he said when the candle my grandfather had lit was half burned. "I'm an old man, not the best company for a young woman like yourself. And you still have a lot to do in this city."

I gave him another hug, and as soon as a surge of protest left his lips, I smiled and walked out of the house.

The sun had set, and the streets had cleared. A few slaves were still running on some late errands. A pang of pride touched my chest knowing that some arrogant lord would have a few slaves less to torture. I walked through the streets, jumping over the cracks as when I was a child. I took a few wrong turns, disappointed with how my knowledge of the streets of Query has dimmed with time. But when I reached the house I used to climb, I found the holds with ease. I fell over the edge and had to catch my breath. Climbing walls wasn't as easy now as it was when I was half my height and weight.

When I could breathe again, I walked across the tiles to the roof I used to spend whole nights on. The view hadn't changed, and I dropped in a seat on the cornice, my gaze running over the curved domes and heavy columns of the Highest Temple.

"Look who came to visit," the young man who sat next to me said.

"It's been too long," I said extending my hand, and he clapped it twice.

"Sorry, I'm late," he said, taking something out

from the folds of his shirt. "These are hard to find these days."

He passed me one of the bundles, and the rich smell of spices hit my nose. I unwrapped the wax paper, and my mouth watered at the sight.

"I'm so happy you carried it close to your heart."

"If you don't want it, I can eat two."

"No, not a chance!" I took a bite before he could steal it from me.

We ate in silence, observing the priest walking on his staff. New ornaments had been added to it, making it grow in volume.

"How does he manage to carry it around?" I asked swallowing the last of the sandwich. "It looks heavier than he is."

"In a few turns, he will have to drag it behind him on a cart..."

"You two are still at odds, aren't you?"

"He prefers to get his boots licked, and I am still a dark spot in his life," Koen said with a shrug.

"About that," I said turning to him. "You either stop stalking my grandfather, or you get much better at it."

Koen chuckled and fell back on the roof. "That man is a mystery. I can lift a purse from a merchant with whom I'm talking, I can come into a house and spend the night in the same room as my mark and no one will notice. But Ragnol... He knows."

"I can introduce you. He might be willing to share some of his secrets."

"I might take you up on that."

"What did you want from him?" I asked.

Koen picked between his teeth with a nail from his little finger and clicked his tongue. "I wanted to be the first one to know when you would be coming back."

"Did you miss me that much?" I asked with laughter on my lips.

"Maybe... But a faction in this city is growing in power. The muscles bought with the coin. The cutthroats greedy for gold and blood. You get the gist of it. The reason I'm telling you this is that they have recently accepted a big contract."

"Why does it feel like I won't enjoy what you have to say?"

"Because the offer comes from Donovan," Koen answered, playing with the ball of paper. He passed it from one hand to another. It disappeared, and he took it out from his sleeve. "You are the mark."

I bit my lip and pulled my knees in a hug.

"Dammit," I muttered. "I came here in search of allies, and yet I meet even more enemies."

"You are smart enough to deal with the enemies by yourself, but I can help you find some allies."

"Who do you have in mind?"

"There is a merchant in this city in the Crimson District," Koen said playing with the paper. "He gives a fair price, no matter who brought the product or its origins... And he is smart enough to not get caught on any of his transactions."

I leaned back, my gaze running over the stars. They had been my constant companion over the past five turns and guided me through the Red Sea without failing me even once.

"Can you arrange a meeting?" I asked. "I have something you would appreciate."

"There is no need in payment..."

"Don't say no before you see what I have to offer."

Koen sat up, his eyes searching my face for any hint. Instead of telling him, I stood up and climbed the building down, Koen right behind me. We walked through the silent city without uttering a word. Koen's steps were so quiet that I had to throw a glance over my shoulder now and then to make sure he followed me.

We walked the plank to the ship and the sailors who were left on guard saluted me as we passed.

I guided Koen to my cabin across the deck of the ship, down the stairs, and to the end of the corridor. Before he took his seat, his gaze had studied my room and noticed everything there was to see.

Walking to my cabinet, I picked two glasses and took the bottle of the finest rum I had hidden in one of the drawers. The blend of spices and burned caramel had matured enough to fill the cabin with its perfect perfume as I uncorked the bottle.

Koen nodded and took his glass. We clinked and sipped on the rum, the sweet burn dancing on my tongue.

"In my line of work, having a precise map of the coasts is something of utter importance," I started as Koen set his glass back on the table. "And whenever

I have the chance, I haunt down every available map."

I opened the drawer and took the folded piece of cloth I had found on a merchant's ship, not a turn ago. As I unfolded it on the table, Koen studied the lines and points that marked the canvas. His brows formed a frown, as he studied the fabric. His finger hovered over some of the crossings and the markings next to it, not touching the cloth as if not to smudge the embedded lines.

Koen slumped back into the chair, swallowed everything that was left in his glass, and leaned back again.

"Impossible..." he muttered, rubbing his forehead.

"That's what I thought. But then I remembered some of the stories my grandfather told me... He knows about it."

"Someone would have had to spend turns trying each exit, crossing each of its levels," Koen muttered. "But at the same time, the points of access I know about are all here..."

"That would make it a real copy then."

"This right here," Koen said pointing to the piece of cloth. "This is the most valued thing that you have on your ship, no matter what trinkets you have hidden in the trunks below the deck."

I smiled, drinking in Koen's blushed cheeks and a glint in his eyes.

"This is the map of all the secret underground passages built through the reign of Enriqua. It also shows the complete system of the sewers... And I am not even sure what these dotted lines are."

I filled Koen's glass and leaned back in my chair, sipping on my own drink.

"Why would you give it away?" he asked.

"I sail the sea," I said and shook my head. "I don't run the streets of this city as you do. You will have much more use in it, and you will do something extraordinary with it, I am sure."

"The possibilities are endless," Koen said. His gaze ran over something only visible to him, his mouth moving in a silent conversation going through his mind. Then he stopped and looked at me. "To think I almost lost the possibility to have this in my possession..."

"I am glad you see how stupid that was," I said.

Koen chuckled, and I lifted my glass. He clanked, a smile still dancing on his lips, and we swallowed the burning liquid down.

***

"A map that would help a man to pass unnoticed in a city filled with guards," the man said and shook his head.

"A wonderful present, don't you think?"

"Where did you get it?"

Isabella shrugged. "On one of the raids we had in the sea. Some merchant had it its trunk. He offered it to me in exchange for his life."

"Did you keep your end of the deal?"

"Of course! Who do you think I am?"

"I don't make assumptions," the man said, checking his parchment. "Who was that merchant?"

"No one of interest or importance. Or so I thought. When I figured what it was, we went back, but the merchant was gone. The ship, a lifeless shell."

"You had no regrets in giving away this treasure?"

"A trade is a trade... A speckle of dust for me, a whole world of opportunities for Koen."

CHAPTER 11

NEW ALLIES

"Was Iblon that ally?" the man asked.

Isabella nodded.

"You didn't like him?"

"He was my associate!"

"That doesn't answer my question."

Isabella huffed and clicked her tongue. "Iblon has his standards, and our opinions didn't always coincide. But that man is like a brother to me and in a certain way he is."

The man nodded and picked his quill. "Tell me about your first meeting."

The morning light came through the window, and I gasped. My head pulsed with pain, and nausea ravaged through my stomach. I sat up and the next wave hit me even harder than before.

I pulled the blanket off and walked to the door. The walls tilted around me. The sea was in unrest. All my muscles protested to the tiniest of my movements. Another wave of nausea hit me, and I had to swallow hard to keep my stomach from emptying its contents.

A figure sat at the table, his fingers looping thread to form a basket. I had to narrow my eyes to see through the fog.

"Pop," I muttered. "What are you doing here?"

"Where do you want me to be except at my own home?"

The room kept swirling around me as I walked to the table and anchored myself in one of the chairs.

"How did I get here?" I asked, squinting as my grandfather shuffled to one of the cupboards and took a sealed jar with some murky liquid inside.

"Koen brought you in here."

"You are on a first-name basis now?"

"He seems like a smart man. We chatted for a while. He had some stories to tell, I had some advice to give."

"Hmm," was the only answer I was able to produce, rubbing on my temples.

Ragnol filled the cup with the liquid from the jar,

spilling some of it on the counter.

"Here, drink this."

I sniffed the cup. The rich smell of herbs forced yet another wave of nausea on me, and I coughed.

"Did I say to smell it?" my grandfather gestured for me to drink it up. "Come on, you have to drink it all in."

I gulped the viscous liquid and had to force myself to keep it down.

"Looking at your face, someone would say that I am trying to poison you."

"It feels like it," I said drying my lips with a cuff of my shirt.

"It can't be as bad as that headache you must be dealing with," my grandfather said.

I winced but didn't answer, slumping my head on the table where I spent the rest of the day, battling vertigo and nausea. My grandfather's concoction helped with both but didn't remedy my pressing headache.

A knock on the door made me sit straight. A wince showed on my face as the blood rushed to my head. Koen walked into the kitchen after Ragnol let him in. His steps resounded in my head, and their voices boomed through my mind as they exchanged a few words in a whisper.

When they were done, I followed Koen outside, shielding my eyes from the heavy light. I folded the scarf around my face, rubbed my temples but followed Koen without a protest or a remark.

"You don't look well." Koen chuckled.

I grunted in an answer, amazed at how he could walk with so much energy, even a spring in his step.

We crossed the busy city in silence. Koen switched his gaze from one possible target to another, even if no one would find himself missing a pouch or a jeweled ring. My attention captured by the paved road in front of me.

We turned around a corner and crossed the invisible frontier with the Crimson District. The houses got replaced by shops and taverns. The streets were cleaner than in the rest of the city, but the nobles that traveled through the district hid behind curtains of their carriages. No one wanted to be spotted in the Crimson District, even though everyone craved to visit it.

We stopped in front of The Voiceless Parrot. The tavern wasn't the best one in Query, but if someone wanted to conduct any business that wasn't official, its secluded compartments offered enough privacy to its visitants.

Koen stepped closer and opened the door for me. I walked inside, my gaze sliding over the opaque curtains to the left and right.

A servant boy approached with a nod.

"Can I help you?"

"We are here to see someone," Koen started.

"Might I have a name?"

"Yamateo."

The boy checked a list in his hands and lifted his gaze back to us again.

"Follow me," he said.

We wove through passages that cut the tavern in small compartments, allowing us to see only the contours of the figures inside. We stopped in front of one of a dozen identical compartments. The serving boy parted a curtain for us, and we slipped inside. Lush cushions filled the space around a low table. A man sat with crossed legs on one side of the table, and before the boy left, he clicked his fingers twice.

"Bring another plate of this and don't forget a refill for me and a beverage for these two," the man said.

The boy bowed and slid the curtain back in place, muffling any noise from the outside and shielding us from view.

"Welcome, dear guests," the man said stretching his palms. "Iblon Yamateo is my name. I guess you are Koen. But might I ask who are you?"

Iblon's gaze landed on me, and I unfolded the scarf covering my face.

"Captain Isabella, at your service."

The man nodded but didn't add anything as the serving boy showed again and set a plate with candied fruits on it and three steaming cups. As the curtains slid back in place, Iblon leaned closer to the table, his belly straining his loosely tied toga. He picked the candied orange and licked his fingers.

"What can I help you with?"

"The word is you buy rare items," I said, picking the cup and sipping on the spiced cha, my stomach grateful for the liquid.

"I might..."

"In that case, I have a few to sell."

Iblon smiled and twisted a gemmed ring around his finger.

"Do you have a sample?" he asked.

I unhooked a leather pouch from my belt and dropped a set of jewels on the table. A sapphire ring encircled in gold fell next to a brooch speckled with diamonds. Iblon brought his fingers to his lips, the smile slipping from his face. He leaned closer before lifting his head to me.

"May I?" he asked pointing at the ring.

"Go ahead."

The merchant took out a set of lenses that lay hidden under his toga and put it to his eye. He examined the jewelry from each side before putting it down. He muttered something to himself and then picked the brooch.

Iblon let it fall on the table and leaned back, dropping the lenses down. "That's where it gets difficult."

I arched a brow. The merchant rubbed his palms in circles, his gaze lost.

"Is there a problem?" Koen asked.

"You see, there is a silent agreement among the merchants if they don't want to fall in disgrace with a very powerful man."

"What agreement?" I asked narrowing my eyes.

"He has forbidden any merchant in Query to strike deals with a certain captain," his gaze finally found me and held it for a long while.

My headache was gone now. I narrowed my eyes,

my fingers twitching to grab the pistol from my belt. Koen put a hand on my arm and Iblon's eyes flickered with interest.

The merchant cleared his throat and said, "I don't have as much information as our friend here, but I can put two and two together. You are his daughter, the one who stole the Golden Eagle."

I cursed under my breath and leaned forward to put the jewels back into the pouch.

"Now, let's not rush anything, shall we?" Iblon said putting his hand on mine. "I'm not much of a stickler for rules."

"But you want something," Koen said. "Something important."

Iblon smiled. "I want exclusivity."

I smirked and shook my head. "You want me to sell everything I find to you?"

"Not everything," Iblon said. "But if you stumble on any jewels like these, they will all come to me. And I will offer you a fair price."

"What's so important about these?" I asked.

"You found them across the sea."

"And?"

"The gnomes had cut these..." Iblon said, picking the ring again. "No matter how great and rich our empire is, no one in all Luganda has this level of craftsmanship. All the gems will have a chip here or a scratch there. But what the gnomes craft in their cave cities... It's priceless for the nobles on this side of the sea."

I shot a glance at Koen, and he answered with a

shrug.

"Fine," I said. "But I have a rule too."

Iblon picked a candied skin of watermelon and sucked on it.

"You never strike any deals with my father."

"That's fair," Iblon said with a chuckle.

He took out a block of paper, punctured in two places and tied with a leather cord. He scribbled something on the paper, tore it out of the block, and passed it to me.

"Go see the Lifespark Holding Company. They will draw this sum from my credit," he said.

I folded the paper and slipped it in the pocket of my trousers.

"It was nice doing business with you," I said, standing up and picking a date from the dish. "We'll see each other soon."

Koen and I walked out of the tavern. I jumped in his arms, and he wrapped them around me.

"I suppose that means thank you."

I chuckled stepping away. "I'm happy to have some good news. Do you blame me?"

Koen smiled and offered me his hand.

"I have some things to do. See you around, sister," he said and we clapped hands.

***

"What's a Lifespark Holding Company?"

"It's a banking system," Isabella answered. When

the frown didn't disappear from the man's face, she added, "I always forget you don't have anything like that here."

"What is it?"

"These friends of Iblon's had this idea. What if you had to travel across Luganda but was afraid of raiders? So, they devised this system. You give your money to a person you know. They would issue you a note, and then after you reach the city you need, you come to the shop with the same name, present your note, and they hand over your money back to you. Except for a small tax of course."

"Thus the Holding Company. But Lifespark?"

"Their last name was Lifespark."

The man nodded for a second, formulating in his head the information Isabella offered him.

CHAPTER 12
SHORT LIVED VICTORY

The man cleared his throat. "From what I gather, this wasn't a very happy day."

Isabella took a deep breath.

"The day was exciting... The night not so much."

"Tell me what happened."

Isabella shook her head and took another deep breath.

"Do you want to finish this another day?"

"No. It has to be told."

***

I strolled home with a wide smile, but it left my lips as soon as I walked through the door.

A storm had crossed the kitchen. Chairs lay scattered across the room. The table was split in two as if someone has landed on it with his back. Some of the cupboards had lost their doors and hung tilted to the side.

I stepped back out into the street and caught the hand of the first urchin I saw.

"Let me go," the boy whimpered.

"Here," I said, wrapping his fingers around a silver coin. "Run to the Singing Buccaneer as fast as you can. Find a man named Aren. Tell him his captain needs him, and he will give you another one."

The boy's eyes were as wide as the coin in his palm.

"Go!"

The boy nodded and rushed through the crowd to the tavern I had mentioned.

I chewed on my lip and walked back into the kitchen. My heart thumped in my chest as I looked around, noticing the spilled milk still dripping from the counter down on the floor. An empty copper pot set on the stove let out a column of smoke, the water for the cha no longer in it. I pushed the pot away from the stove with a rag and threw a look around.

Something came crashing down on the floor in my grandfather's room. I took one of my pistols out and tiptoed across the kitchen.

My back to the wall, I pushed the door open. A

shadow dashed across the room. I took a deep breath, cocked the hammer, and stepped inside.

The storm had found its way into my grandfather's room. The curtains flapped with the evening breeze over an opened window. Desk drawers lay scattered on the floor next to a fallen chair and a broken vase.

A moan came from somewhere in the shadows. I stepped closer, my eyes searching for the source of the cry for help. My gaze landed on the figure of my grandfather sprawled on the floor. My pistol fell from my hand. Before it landed on the floor with a loud clank, I was on my knees, cradling my grandfather on my lap.

Blood oozed from the wound at the back of his head, but he still breathed. Tears formed in my eyes, and I had to blink them away. I looked around in search of anything that could help, and my eyes met with Aren's.

"What happened?!"

"I don't know," I said, shaking my head.

"Is he alive?"

"Yes, but I don't know for how much time... Please, go get a priest!"

Aren turned on his heels.

"Not the priest of a Highest Temple," I said, and Aren threw me a look over his shoulder. "A temple of Eluvia is hidden in a house three streets to the east from here."

Aren didn't ask any questions. He nodded and left. I was alone again, my grandfather cradled in my lap. I tore a piece from the sheet that lay crumpled on the floor and pressed it to the wound. The blood drenched it in an instant, seeping through my fingers and staining my clothes.

As moments passed, Ragnol's breathing became shallow.

"Please... please, hold on," I muttered. "The priest will be here soon."

An eternity has passed before the door opened, and Terrace walked into the room. He didn't have a mantle or an ornate staff. Only an insignia of a sparkle of light marked him as a priest of the temple of Eluvia.

Terrace dropped to his knees next to me. He passed his hands over Ragnol's body and then over his head, a glow spreading around.

"Set him down, Isabella," he said, taking out a satchel tied with a leather cord.

I did as he ordered, and Aren wrapped a hand around my shoulder. Terrace spread the white powder from the pouch over Ragnol's wound. His hands kept hovering over his head as his lips moved with a silent incantation.

The flow of blood stopped, and Terrace leaned back.

"I did what I could..." The priest looked up to me. "I will not tell you to pray for his recovery..."

Tears spilled down my cheeks, and I closed my eyes.

"I am not sure he will live through the night..." The priest walked closer and put a hand on my shoulder. "He might wake up, Isabella. But I can't promise that. I will stay here and make sure he is in as little pain as possible."

"Thank you, Terrace..." I said swallowing down a lump in my throat.

He nodded and with the help from Aren lifted my grandfather's body on the bed.

I walked out of the room and into the kitchen. I leaned on the wall, my gaze lost on the crimson and charcoal spots on the ceiling. Aren walked into the room and took me out of my stupor.

"There is something you should see..." he said.

I followed him into the room that had been my father's. In black paint, crooked letters covered the walls.

Usurper.

Traitor.

Murderer.

The words have been written time and again.

The door to the house opened, and someone walked into the room. I turned to see Koen stop in his tracks, his gaze running over the wreckage and debris.

"Isabella..." Koen said, his eyes finding mine. "Donovan's Crimson Storm just landed in the port."

***

"That's a strange coincidence," the man said.

"I've told you this once. No such things as coincidences exist."

"Let's hear it then."

"The rebels of the Pirate King's regime knew my father was coming. They wanted to see him suffer."

"But it was you who found Ragnol."

"Yes," Isabella said with a sigh. "That wasn't supposed to happen. I wasn't supposed to be in Query."

"Didn't you want to hide from your father?"

"At that moment... I didn't want to do anything except to be there for my pop the same way he has been there all my life."

***

I walked back into the kitchen, Koen and Aren fast on my heels.

"What in the world happened here?" Koen asked.

My gaze wandered over the same things they saw. The broken furniture, the shuttered glasses and dishes.

"Your guess is as good as mine…"

"Well," Koen said. "It might take him some time, but he will be here soon."

"Leave, both of you."

"Captain?"

"Aren, don't make me repeat myself."

"Are you sure about it?" Koen asked.

"It's time we've met again."

Koen sighed and nodded.

"Good luck, friend," he said offering me his hand.

I clapped it twice, and Koen followed Aren out of the house.

I picked one of the chairs, straightened it, and sat down. My elbows on my thighs, I put my head in my hands and tried to swallow down the tears which kept coming.

The door opened, and I sat up. A man in his forties stood in the entrance. The light on top of the door drew a hallo around his head against the dark sky. Donovan walked in, each of his steps echoing through the empty space.

"Well, girl. Did you come to pay for your sins?"

I smirked, the rage burning through my veins.

"Look around," I murmured, filling each of my words with hatred. "Or do you have no space left in your heart for anyone but yourself?"

"Did you decide to throw another one of your tantrums?"

I jumped to my feet, my finger pointing to his old room.

"This one might hit closer to you and your deeds than you might be thinking!"

My father narrowed his eyes but walked into the room I had pointed. I followed him, swallowing down the lump that had formed in my throat.

"There is more," I muttered.

Donovan turned to me, his nostrils flaring.

"Pop… He got hit…" I started.

"Where is he?!"

"He's in his room. I paid for a priest…"

Donovan was no longer listening. He pushed me

aside and ran into Ragnol's room. I followed suit.

Terrace had cleaned as much blood as he could and straightened some of the broken furniture. He sat on a chair next to the bed. My grandfather's feeble body lay covered with a thick blanket. His face had become ashen, and I turned my gaze away, not wanting to have this memory in my mind.

My father's gaze turned to me again. "Have you seen who did this?"

"When I came home, they were gone."

"Come, let's talk," he gestured for me to follow him when Terrace motioned for us to be quiet.

Donovan walked across the room to a cupboard, its door hanging on only one of its hinges. He took two metal cups and a bottle of a strong spirit that had survived the attack. I sat on another straightened chair, my shoulders slumped. He took the seat next to me, filled both cups, and passed me one of them. We gulped down the burning spirit without clanking nor saying a word.

"We can have a truce while we solve this," Donovan finally said, his gaze set on the bottom of his cup.

I didn't have any strength to answer him. All the anger I harbored drenched with the recent events. Instead, I finished what was left in my cup and picked the bottle to refill. We sat in the center of the storm, each one of us drowning our sorrows in the burning spirit.

The first light of the day seeped into the room when Terrace walked into the kitchen. He didn't have to say anything. We both knew what had happened. I sobbed and covered my face as burning tears streamed down my cheeks. Donovan put a hand on my shoulder, and I didn't shake it, searching for any comfort I could get.

He went into the room and stayed there while I downed a few more glasses of spirit which didn't bring the numbness I sought.

My father rubbed his bloodshot eyes as he walked back into the kitchen and closer to the priest.

"When can we have the ceremony, Terrace?"

"I can send someone to prepare him during the day," Terrace said. "And we can have the ceremony tomorrow."

Donovan nodded, "How much do we owe you?"

"Your daughter paid more than enough," he said. "I will let you two alone."

Terrace walked out, and I rubbed my eyes, trying to fend the tears away.

"I will pay you back."

"Don't," I shook my head.

"When I left, I promised you I would keep you safe, that I will not let any of you two suffer the same fate Yana did."

"Yet another promise you won't keep," I said with a shrug.

"Isa…"

"We might be in a truce, but I don't have to talk to you," I said standing up. "One more thing, I know it's hard for you to think about anything else but yourself. But I asked you to call me Isabella."

"I'm sorry, Isabella," he said. "Don't go. This was always your home. I have some things to deal with anyway."

He readjusted his black leather vest and walked out of the house, leaving me alone.

When the man Terrace sent showed up at the door, I had finished the bottle. He eyed the havoc that reigned in the house but followed me into my grandfather's room without a word. I didn't step inside, unable to see Ragnol the way he was now. His body broken, his spirit gone.

While he worked, I took in the broken house. I sighed and rolled up the sleeves of my bloodied shirt. I picked a bucket filled with water, mixed some soap into it, and with a brush in my hand walked into my father's room. Sweat rolled down my back and mixed into the blood that stained my shirt as I rubbed the words that I knew were true.

When the walls were spotless again, I picked all the debris and broken furniture and put it into a cart I ordered with another urchin. When that was done, I went through the broken dishes and jars, salvaging anything that was still worth it, throwing away the rest.

The man from the temple was gone, but I still worked, fixing the shelves and cupboards that I could or discarding the ones that weren't worth it. I changed the linen in my father's room and mine, throwing the old ones away. But I couldn't bring myself to cross the door frame into my grandfather's room.

When night fell, only the missing furniture could tell someone had ransacked the house. The dark thoughts crept into my mind again, and I could no longer chase them away.

I went into my room and slipped into my old bed, finding no longer any comfort in it. The tears came again, and I cried myself to sleep.

I woke with the touch of the sun on my face. Donovan was in the kitchen, standing over a steaming pot on the stove.

He picked a spoon and put some of its contents into the last dish left unbroken. He pushed the plate across the counter in my direction, pulled another spoon from a drawer, and picked some of the food directly from the pot. I nibbled at the undercooked porridge that somehow tasted of burned milk, but it wasn't the flavor of it that brought nausea to my lips.

"You should wash and change," Donovan said, putting the pot back on the counter, a scowl on his face. "The ceremony will start soon."

I nodded and abandoned the untouched food on the counter. No strength left in me to heat it up, I washed with cold water. Back into my room, I looked around, my hair leaving wet traces on my skin. I knew I wouldn't be able to spend another day or night here.

My father hadn't moved from where he stood next to a pot with the spoiled food.

"I won't be coming back here," I said putting my bag down.

"Me neither."

"You should sell the house then."

His gaze went to mine, his blue eyes burrowing into the brown of mines. Before they slid to my waist where his pistols were holstered over my mother's favorite blue satin scarf.

"I will take care of it before I leave," he said, his eyes climbing back to my face and a sigh leaving his lips.

I nodded and sat on one of the chairs. My father took the other one but faced away from me. When our gazes met, each one of us looked the other way.

A few men came into the house, and my father jumped to his feet to show him to my grandfather's room. When they walked out, Ragnol's body on their shoulders, I turned my gaze away.

Donovan and I followed the men through the crowded streets and inside the small temple to Eluvia. My gaze ran over the crowd that had gathered for the ceremony.

Some of the neighbors Ragnol was close with sat in the first rows of the temple that praised the god they didn't believe in. The crew of the Golden Eagle stood at the back. Koen and even Iblon had merged with the crowd. A few cloaked desert wanderers stood next to my men, but most of the hundreds of people in the temple I didn't recognize.

My father let out a shallow breath when his eyes ran over the crowd, but after a short pause, he walked to the first row. Terrace climbed the steps as soon as I settled next to my father.

"We gather here today to honor a friend to us all," he started. "But I don't need to tell you what good has this man done or what loss his passing will bring. I want you to remember him as you walk the paths of your life and let him live in your memories."

Terrace smiled at me and Donovan before adding, "And I want you to remember what good he has done and try to live by his tenets."

The man who had prepared Ragnol's body brought a torch, and Terrace set the ceremonial pyre on fire. The temple stayed silent as the fire devoured my grandfather's body, and his soul left to meet Kesareth on her island.

One by one people dispersed until it was only me and my father left in front of lifeless ashes.

Donovan sighed and stood up. He stopped by my side and put a hand on my shoulder again.

"It was nice seeing you, even if the reason for it wasn't perfect."

I didn't answer, unable to find the words. My father walked to the exit, his boots echoing in an empty temple.

"The truce will be over as soon as one of us leaves the port," he said, without turning to me. "You might have made friends and forged alliances, but I advise you to be cautious when you sail the Red Sea. My dogs will be keeping an eye out for the Golden Eagle."

***

Isabella rolled her shoulders back.

"Was that a threat?" the man asked.

"In a way," Isabella said with a smirk. "But at the same time, he wanted me to understand something."

"What is that exactly?"

"Our little war was far from over."

The man nodded and picked another parchment.

"What happened to those who did that to your house?"

"My father killed them. Isn't that obvious?"

The man looked up at Isabella from the parchment in front of him. "I don't presume things. Do you have more details?"

"He took them into the sea and tied them to the masts of his ship until they were half-mad from the constant sun and wind, thirst and hunger. And then made them walk the plank each with a pistol with one bullet in it." The man wrote Isabella's words down. "From what I heard, the shots were fired even before they fell into the water."

CHAPTER 13

UNEXPECTED ENCOUNTERS

"When was the next time you met Brook?" the man behind the desk asked.

"He tried killing me," Isabella said with a shrug.

"I am sorry?"

Isabella laughed and straightened a non-existent fold of her trousers.

"Well, not personally. But he wanted me to notice him."

"Do tell."

***

I sat on the roof, the locket spinning on its golden chain as I twisted it one way and another. The sun warmed my skin, and the wind brushed some sand through my hair.

"I wasn't expecting you back so soon," Koen said as he climbed to the roof and took a seat next to me.

"A turn has passed. Isn't that long enough?"

Koen nodded.

"Here," he said offering me a small box.

"Another trade?"

"If you wish it to be so," he said.

I opened the box and smiled. The black jewel that we have been passing from one to another was set in a platinum rim, a delicate chain coiled back from it.

"When I gave it to you all that time ago, I traded it for an answer to a question. But I hoped to find a friend, and I did," he said. "It belongs to you."

I smiled and picked the necklace up and slid it over my head next to the golden locket.

"This is so sentimental of you," I said nudging him in the ribs.

"You tell anyone, and I will kill you."

"I guess it wouldn't be a real friendship without a life threat now and then," I said laughter dancing on my lips.

"So," Koen said when I stopped. "What brings you to this beautiful city?"

"My first mate has pointed out to me that my crew has to see the land for enough time to crave the sea even more. And I had some jewels to sell. Iblon was ecstatic."

Koen nodded.

"How is your treasure hunt going on?"

"The underground passages are a treasure of its own," Koen said with a shrug. "But I hadn't had time lately."

I arched a brow.

"I have recruited a few men and women," he said. "We have a small organization growing, and a few contracts are in need to be filled."

We sat on our roof as the day passed and talked about Koen's guild and my adventures. About the priest of the Highest Temple and his intrigues, about Donovan the Eagle and his dogs. When the stars dotted the sky, a yawn escaped my mouth.

"It's time to call it a night," Koen said.

I nodded and climbed to my feet.

With another clap of hands, we parted ways. I walked the empty streets and breathed in the cool air. A shuffle of feet came from behind me. Another servant on some late-night errand, or a worker returning home after an evening spent in the tavern.

I turned a corner, and a few shadows disappeared at the other end of the street. I stopped in my tracks, my eyes narrowed. I looked over my shoulder, but whoever walked the deserted streets of Query behind my back had stopped too.

I started walking again, and the sound of the steps

came to my ears again. I put my hand on the belt, my fingers hooked next to the pistols and one of the daggers.

As I reached the middle of the alley, two figures stepped from the shadows where they had gone into before. I threw a look over my shoulder and saw the owners of the shuffling feet behind me.

I stopped walking, letting the men come closer. Spiked bats and sharpened knives appeared in their hands.

"Hello, boys," I said, rolling my neck. "To what do I owe the pleasure of this meeting?"

None of them answered as they circled me up. One of the men leaped at me, but I took my dagger in a flash and let it fly. The man ducked, but too late. The blade slashed his neck. His wound gushed blood onto the cobbled alley.

The owners of the shuffling feet moved as one. Their spiked bats went behind their backs with a threatening swing. I rolled away and picked my dagger from the ground.

The bats smashed the wall with a powerful blow. Bits of stone and wood rained over me. I took the other dagger out from my boot and retreated as the men had swung their bats at me. The third man with a knife of his own slashed at me. I ducked, but the blade grazed the skin of my shoulder.

"Dammit! I liked that shirt!" I cried.

I struck the blade into the back of one of the bat owners. He tried to reach it with his thick fingers, his body losing strength.

"Let me help you with that," I said and pulled the dagger out with a spray of blood.

The man with the dagger slashed his weapon at me as the one with the bat swung it behind his back again. I carved the unprotected belly of the second bat owner, cutting through cloth, skin, and muscle. He let the bat fall and followed his companion to the ground.

The last of my opponents spat and switched his hold on the dagger. I rushed at him, pointing my blades at his belly. The man ducked and sprung his own weapon forward, and I smiled.

With another step and a pirouette, I kicked the dagger from his hand and run my blades into his shoulders. The man whimpered, as I pressed harder, pinning him to the wall. Blood oozed from his wounds.

"Who sent you?"

"You have a black mark set on you," the man spat each of his words. "Figure it out."

"None of you are from are a pirate ship. This is something else…"

The man swallowed and closed his eyes.

"Come on, you know I'll pull it out from you. Tell me what you know, and the pain will be gone."

"Brook is our leader," the man whispered, climbing to his toes to relieve the pressure of the blades.

"That name rings a bell… Brook what?"

"Brook Carreiro," the man said wincing. "Let me go."

"Not yet. Where can I find him?"

"Our group gathers in The Drunk Moon…"

"Perfect," I said taking one of the daggers out. "Now, guide me to it."

The man's eyes widened.

"He will kill me!"

"He might," I said with a nod. "But if you don't, I will."

The man gulped and seemed to think about it for a moment.

"Just take this out," he said pointing to my other dagger.

I smiled and took it out. The man cried out and dropped to his knees. After a second, he climbed to his feet again. The mercenary dragged his feet to the tavern, clutching his shoulders. He stole a few gazes at me, but my blade at his kidneys dissuaded him from whatever was on his mind.

My own shoulder prickled with pain. My fingers came away crimson and wet as I touched the gush he had given me. A few beads of sweat formed on my forehead even on such a cold night.

The man guided me across the city away from the Highest Temple and the port, closer to the wall that surrounded Query. He stopped next to a tavern and pointed to the door.

I threw a gaze around. The buildings around us were not inhabited. Or at least someone wanted them to look that way as I caught a glimpse of a movement in one of the broken windows.

"After you," I pressed my dagger harder at the

mercenary's hip.

The man spat, shook his head, and opened the door. We walked into a filled with tobacco smoke room. The music stopped, and all the conversations around the tables died.

Before anyone could react, I pushed the man to the ground, and he stayed down. My boot on his back, I took out my pistol, cocked the hammer and pointed it at his head. I ran my eyes over the faces that looked at me. Some of them were set in a growl, others in a wild smirk, but all of them showed hostility.

"I have an appointment with Brook Carreiro," I said. "Anyone can point me in his direction?"

One of the faces had a crooked smile spreading on its lips. A smile that brushed my mind with a memory of something long forgotten. A man in his twenties stood up and walked close to me.

"Isabella Dromandor! I thought you would never come."

"One and only," I answered, my gun climbing up to the chest of the man in front of me.

A few men around the room stood up, drawing their weapons. Brook lifted a hand. As one, the men followed a silent order. They stopped in their movements, dropped their hands to their sides, and slid back into their seats.

"Follow me," he whispered and turning on his heels added to the room. "Someone, take Orlin to a medic before he bleeds in my tavern. And where is the music? This isn't a funeral!"

The bard next to the fireplace strung the chords

of his lute, and the conversations resumed at the tables. As we walked to the room in the back, the men followed our passage with their gazes. A few climbed to their feet to help Orlin with his wounds but most kept staring at the pistol in my hand.

Walking into the small room at the back, I tried to do what Koen always did. But where he noticed possibilities and routes of escape, I only saw bricked windows and obstructed doors. Brook closed the door behind us and offered me a seat.

"Do you need something for that?" he asked, pointing at my shoulder.

"No, I prefer to stain as much of your furniture as possible."

"Can you at least put that relic in your holster?"

"Then how am I supposed to shoot you if you try anything funny?"

Brook chuckled and shook his head.

"Rum, I suppose," he said walking towards a shelf filled with bottles made of thick glass.

"Yes, unless you plan to poison me. Then I'll pass."

Brook chuckled again, his eyes twinkling in the candlelight. He put my drink in front of me and filled a glass for himself from the same bottle. His crooked smile not leaving his lips, his eyes on mine, he took the opposite seat and sipped on his drink.

"Might I offer a deal?"

"Might I be blunt?"

"You were holding back?"

I shrugged, and a wince broke on my face. Brook

looked at the trickle of blood escaping from my wound and sliding down my arm before pooling around my hand on the couch.

"Well, by all means. Before you bleed to death, what is that you wanted to say?" he said leaning across the low table.

"You tried to kill me, not an hour ago. Why would I want to strike a deal with you?"

"I wanted to claim your attention, which worked out perfectly, don't you think?" he asked, crossing one leg over the other and downing his drink.

I chuckled and sipped on my rum.

"The four dimwicks that I sent after you were the stupidest of the lot."

"They ruined my shirt," I said.

Brook's smile widened, and he shook his head. A pleasant shiver ran across my skin as his eyes found mine again.

"I will buy you a new one."

I shook my head and stood up, setting the unfinished glass on the table.

"I am tired and in no mood for this. Next time, send a note."

Brook set his own glass and walked close to me.

"You won't even hear it?" he whispered into my ear.

I hit him in his jaw, and Brook stumbled back. He rubbed the place where my knuckles had met his skin. The crooked smile danced on his lips, showing rows of white teeth.

"I said: send a note."

I turned on my heels and walked away, resisting the urge to run out of the inn. As far away as my feet would take me.

***

"Why didn't you kill him?"

"Why would I?" Isabella asked with a frown. "Do you think I am some kind of merciless assassin?"

"Didn't you consider him a threat?"

"He could be," Isabella said with a shrug. "But he wasn't. And even if he were, I wouldn't kill a man just because he crossed my path."

"That's not what I understood from all the combat you had in the sea."

"That's different."

"Is it though?" the man asked dropping his quill. "Or did you let it slide because you liked him?"

Isabella smiled and leaned in her seat.

"I had no trouble going against my father. Why do you think I would take in account an attraction when the life of my crew... my life, would be on the line?"

The man gave Isabella a reserved smile and moved a parchment to the growing pile on his desk.

CHAPTER 14

THE BROTHERHOOD OF FOUR

The man pulled a parchment from a drawer of his desk, ran over lines of text with his eyes, and lifted his gaze to Isabella.

"When did you meet Brook the next time?"

"When he offered me something I couldn't refuse."

"And you still had no recollection of your first meeting?"

"That day is still hidden behind a thick veil. I don't know what that magician has done to me. The only thing I remember is flashes of everything that happened."

The man picked his quill and took a fresh parchment.

"Tell me about his offer"

***

I sat at one of the tables in the Singing Buccaneer. Aren had a tankard in front of him, but as per tradition, he had yet to touch it. Some of the sailors were still sleeping off their drinking from the last night, others had already found their way into the tavern and spread around the room with a game of cards, dice, or knuckles.

An urchin walked through the main door and wove across the room filled with drunken men and half-dressed serving girls towards our table.

"A message for the lady," he said passing me a folded parchment.

I sighed and slipped a copper into the boy's palm. The urchin pulled down his hat and rushed out of the tavern.

"Someone is trying really hard," Aren muttered over his drink.

"Shut it."

I unfolded the parchment and read the note.

Don't you think this is getting ridiculous? You've asked for a note. I've sent you ten already.

Come to The Drunk Moon, let's talk.

The man who makes you laugh

I shook my head and put the note in the pocket of my trousers.

"Give the lad a chance," Aren said.

"Didn't I ask you to stop talking?"

"Yeah, well, sometimes you won't listen to reason. Do I have to let you run into a brick wall?"

"This is not what you think it is," I said picking my cup.

"Sure. I might miss some details, but I'm not dumb."

I knew Aren was right. I wasn't returning any notes Brook had sent me because of how he made my skin tingle with excitement. And how his smile made me want to smile back.

I did need allies though, in the turn we had been in the sea we've run into three ships of my father's fleet. One of the battles almost ended with the Golden Eagle at the bottom of the Red Sea.

"Alright," I said draining the glass in my hand. I picked my pistols, checked if they were loaded, and slid them back into the holster. "The man wants to talk… I'll listen."

"Good luck," Aren said and pressed his lips to the tankard.

"I don't need it."

"He might," he said with a chuckle.

"Do me a favor in the meantime."

"Sure thing, captain."

"Finish that drink of yours, ask for another one. Who knows? Maybe you will loosen up a little for the first time in your life."

"And who will watch over your sorry crew."

I shook my head and left the Singing Buccaneer. Instead of walking straight ahead, I took a long route around. Everything to avoid my old house and the memories it brought. Some of the men and women stole glances of me; I wasn't one who blended well with the crowd. The Golden Eagle and the Red Sea were my home, not Query.

Close to the Drunk Moon, the streets got emptier, the building still vacant. But the men with pieces of armor and mean-looking weapons at their belts stared me down as I crossed the streets. Some of the men flexed their muscles, some of the women threw me stares as sharp as daggers.

I opened the door of the Drunk Moon and walked inside. All the noise, music, and conversations died in an instant.

"You walked into a wrong tavern, girl," one of the men closest to the door said. "Leave before I have to show you the way out."

"Watch whom you call girl," I said, caressing the pistol with my thumb. "Or didn't they tell you what happened to the last one who tried?"

Brook walked into the room, deep in a conversation with a woman at his side. I felt a pang in my chest and had to roll my shoulders back to dismiss the feeling I discovered was jealousy.

Brook stopped, threw a gaze around the room in search of the reason for the silence. He found me in an instant, and a smile spread on his lips.

The mercenary in the front seat didn't care who I was and wouldn't take a no for an answer. He sprung to his feet and towered over me, cracking his knuckles.

"Well, it seems that I have to teach you a lesson."

Before he had made a step, I had drawn my dagger out and moved closer. My blade dug deep in his belly but didn't break the skin.

"Sit up, Emil," Brook's voices boomed through the room. "Before she shows what she can do with that weapon."

Emil seemed to think about it, a scowl on his face. But then he stepped away and took his seat. The leader of the mercenaries motioned for me to follow him, and I crossed the tavern still plunged in silence.

As soon as the doors closed behind my back in Brook's private room, the music in the main room started to flow again and the conversations regained their previous volume. My host filled two glasses from the same bottle as the last time and took a seat.

"You came," he said, leaning back in one of the armchairs.

I picked the glass but didn't sit down on the new couch. I didn't want to be close to that man, even if the table would break the space between us, it wouldn't be enough to drain the tension.

"I like my men surprised," I said, walking closer to the shelves, reading the labels on the countless bottles spread around the room.

Brook laughed, and a smile spread on my lips. I forced it away as I turned to him again.

"What is the proposition you talked about?" I asked.

"Straight to business," Brook said, putting the glass back on the table. "I like that…"

I shrugged and walked to the armchair, unable to resist the desire to move closer. I didn't sit down but put it as another barrier between us, leaning on it with my arms.

"We have some things in common, and I heard you have friends in other spheres of the same business."

"I won't confirm nor deny that."

"Well. Let's suppose that's true…" Brook said.

I lifted a brow, and Brook reached for his glass again. The cuff of his shirt moved up his arm, revealing patterns of ink dancing on his tanned skin and climbing up and under the cloth. I bit my lip, clutching the glass in my hand even harder. The entwining black lines flashed in my mind, but I couldn't place them. Brook caught my gaze and looked down at his arm. He readjusted the cuff, the patterns hidden below the fabric.

"Imagine the power a collaboration such as ours could have. A band of mercenaries and a plunderer of goods. Now add to that a guild of thieves of secrets and belongings, and last but not least a dealer of rare items."

"If these people existed, you would have to ask

them yourself. Even if I knew them, I couldn't speak for any of them."

"Then it's a good thing I sent a note to each one of them," he said. "I might have something I can offer that any of you won't be able to refuse.

"So, you do know how to write those!"

"I thought you would appreciate the special attention."

I narrowed my eyes and sipped on the rum in my glass.

"What did you offer them?"

"A few tips for the guild I managed to collect and a couple of rare items for the merchant. And don't think I've forgotten you, I have the best proposition of them all."

I arched a brow, playing with the glass in my hand.

"Protection."

I opened my mouth, but Brook put down his glass and walked closer.

"Before you say anything, hear me out. I know you can take care of yourself out in the sea and on the streets. No matter if it's the dogs of the Pirate King or the thugs of Luganda..." he brushed one of my curls behind my ear. "But wouldn't you like to walk the streets of this city without having to throw a look over your shoulder each time you step down from your ship on this side of the sea?"

I mulled over the offer. Query could become a safe harbor for me and my crew. Aren could finally drink his money away instead of surveying my crew and me each time we dropped anchor in this city.

"What do you say?"

"I can't promise you anything before I can hear what the others have to say."

He stretched his hand out, the way the people on the shores of the Allied Kingdom did when offering a handshake.

"I will take this as a yes," he said.

I put my hand in his and shook it. But he didn't let me go, his thumb tracing little circles on the back of my hand, sending waves of heat up my arm and down my body.

"You really don't remember me, do you, iris?" he whispered, his smile gone, his eyes searching mine.

"Should I?"

"We were younger. You ran through the streets of this city as if chased by the bees. I just moved into this town…"

A vague memory pierced through my mind. A black flower, tucked behind my ear, a crooked smile, a kiss under the stars, and a wild promise. Before all the memories of my past burst out, I trampled them down, not ready to deal with those I kept hidden.

"I told you I'd wait."

My heart raced in my chest, my cheeks flustered. My hand was still lodged in his. Brook leaned closer, his breath brushing my skin and my stomach twirled inside me.

His other hand brushed through my hair, and Brook kissed me as I've only been kissed once before, under the sky dotted with stars.

"You remember. At least you do so now," he

whispered, my hand still in his.

He leaned closer, his lips tracing mine. He put another hand behind my head and kissed me again.

***

"Was Brook the one who had the idea for the Brotherhood?" the man asked with lifted brows.

Isabella laughed, "He didn't only have an idea for it; he did all in his power for it to become a reality."

"But how did he know all these things?"

"Do you think that because he was a mercenary, he was stupid?" Isabella asked. "Brook was their leader for a reason... But he had paid a good coin to gather all the things about us."

"Weren't you afraid of the man with such knowledge?"

Isabella smirked, "What Brook had dug up was a fraction of what passed through Koen each turn... No. Each month. So, the answer to your question is no."

"Alright," the man said. "Tell me what the others had to say."

***

I walked into the Singing Parrot, and the serving boy left me waiting at the bar while he checked if Iblon had approved my arrival. We had met dozens of times in this place, but each time I had to tolerate the half-drunken men at the bar. When the boy was back, I followed him with a roll of my eyes. He guided me to the compartment where Koen and Iblon sat on the stitched cushions and sipped on their steaming cups.

"I hate the policy of this place." I dropped to one of the cushions and unhooked my scarf.

"Some enjoy it. Some don't," Iblon said with a shrug. "If you want, we can find another tavern, but it won't be as discrete as this one."

"No, it's fine."

We clapped hands with Koen, and Iblon clicked his fingers. The golden bracelets on his wrists clinked as he moved his hands. The serving boy appeared through the parted curtain, and Iblon ordered another steaming cup for me. At the same time he returned, Brook followed him inside, without waiting for approval from our host.

"Unbelievable! Even the thug gets a free pass?"

"Nice to see you too, iris."

I looked at Koen, searching for a rescue, but he followed each of the newcomer's movements instead.

"Welcome, welcome," Iblon said. "Take a seat."

Brook nodded and dropped into a cross-legged seat at my side, and I turned my head away, trying to hide the fact that we knew each other.

"I suppose you all had time to think about what I had offered you."

I nodded and turned to Koen who looked at me with a smile. After a while, he shrugged. Brook's gaze landed on Iblon.

"Yes," the merchant said rubbing his hands.

"So, might I hear what you have to say about it?"

Koen took out a pouch from his shirt and dropped it on the table. Brook opened it, and a leather-bound parchment fell next to a set of jewels.

"I checked your tips," Koen said. "They are solid. If you can keep them coming, I'm in."

Iblon leaned and looked at the necklace with a grin on his face.

"Who doesn't like filling his pockets with more coin?"

Everyone's gazes turned to me, and I smirked. "This has the potential to be exciting."

Iblon laughed and dropped the necklace back on the table.

"It's done then," Brooke said and looked at me. "But I wouldn't want this to be only about business."

Koen narrowed his gaze, I rolled my eyes, and Iblon chuckled.

"And what do you want?" Iblon asked.

"We will have our part in it," Brook said, picking his cup. "But if one of us will need help, the others will offer it. We will only be strong if we have each other's back."

"What are you saying?" I asked.

"We will be a brotherhood. The four of us will fight side by side and grow richer together," Brook added.

"The Brotherhood of Four," I muttered with a smile.

"I rather like the sound of it, but I'll leave the

fighting to the three of you," Iblon said, lifting his cup with a smile. "To us then."

"To the future," Koen added, lifting his own cup.

"To the new adventures," I said.

"To the Brotherhood of Four," Brook finished.

We clinked our steaming glasses and sipped on the hot tea.

***

"That simple."

Isabella nodded.

"You were a family," the man said with a nod.

"We still are," Isabella said. "No matter what happens, we can always count on each other. And neither of us had ever wronged another."

"I can't imagine things were always smooth."

"They never are, but we always found the means to deal with the troubles that came our way."

"Hm," the man said and scribbled something on the parchment.

CHAPTER 15

INTO THE SEA AGAIN

"What went wrong?"

"What do you mean?" Isabella asked.

"You left. So something didn't work out."

"It's nothing like that."

The man waited for Isabella to go on. When she didn't, he added. "If you thought it would be so exciting, why would you leave?"

Isabella sighed. "It was one big adventure. It still is. But Query... That city had brought too much pain in my life."

I crossed the city from the Singing Buccaneer to the Drunk Moon. The sun slid half-way behind the horizon and allowed some fresh breeze to pass through the city and to cool the streets. I had walked this path more times in the past turn than I had sailed the Red Sea since I had stolen the Golden Eagle.

Some of Brook's thugs nodded at me as I passed by their side, others kept with their things no longer noticing my comings and goings.

Inside the Drunk Moon, I walked across the common room and into the private one in the back. Hundreds of candles spread a warm light through space. It danced on the soft petals of the thousands of irises of different colors that decorated the room. The music from the common room filtered through the walls and added to the atmosphere.

"Did you finally allow Sol to decorate the place?" I asked.

Brook laughed, his shoulders quaking.

"I will do it more often if it's so much to your liking."

I took another look around, noticing Koen and Iblon. Each at one of the armchairs in the corner of the room, they sipped on their drinks, busy with a lively discussion.

"Finally," Iblon said putting his cup down. "We've been waiting for you for at least an hour."

"I wasn't aware we had a meeting... And since

when do we meet in the Drunk Moon, I thought the Silent Parrot was your choice of preference."

Iblon laughed. "We wanted to celebrate, and what better place to do it than in the tavern of the man who had managed to make us become what we are."

Brook offered me a drink as I took a seat on the couch.

"It's not that I don't like to drink… But what are we celebrating?"

"Our associate here," Iblon motioned at Koen. "He managed to put some spies in the palace. It made us remember what we were and the path we had walked. So, we decided to celebrate."

"Here, here," Brook said lifting his glass.

Koen chuckled, and everyone's gaze turned to me.

"Aye to that!" I said lifting my glass.

I forced a smile on my lips but didn't feel the part. We drank and talked and made plans, but my mind wasn't set on the celebration. Iblon was right. We had come a long way. I've managed to double the riches of the Golden Eagle, and we had many more contracts to fulfill than we could deliver. Rare items to smuggle, unauthorized men to transport across the sea, and ships to plunder. But I had made my name in the Red Sea, not in Query. I missed the wind in my hair and the salt in my lungs.

"What's on your mind, iris?" Brook said, sitting up next to me.

I threw my gaze around and noticed that Iblon and Koen had left.

"You weren't really here…" he said running his

hand over my arm.

I bit my lip, and Brook freed it, planting a kiss instead. I smiled and cupped his cheek.

"I have to talk to someone," I said.

"Talk to me."

"We've known each other for a long time, but Koen is the one who can help me here."

"Of course," Brook answered standing up.

I walked back out of the Drunk Moon, the three moons in different phases brightening the sky along with the myriad of stars. The fresh air filled my lungs. A tingle of salt mixed into the smell of the sand-filled city and my heart tugged even more.

I crossed the city and climbed the building so familiar to me. A figure dressed in grey sat on the roof. I dropped next to Koen, and he offered me the sandwich wrapped in the wax paper.

"Never thought you would be walking with one of these in your pocket all day long," I said with a smile.

"I knew you would come. You had that look on your face during the celebration... I saw it once already. When you asked me about Donovan."

"Did everyone notice?"

"Iblon didn't, he isn't very observant for these types of things," Koen said with a shrug. "But I don't have to tell you what's on Brook's mind."

I dug into my sandwich, my full attention on the hot sauce that spread through my mouth. The food in my belly, I fell back on the roof, observing the Northern Spear. Vega twinkled on the dark sky, beckoning me closer.

"When will you leave?" Koen asked.

"How do you always know?"

Koen shook his head. I didn't see it, but I was sure he had a smile on his face.

"This one is easy," he said leaning back, making a pillow with his hands. "You miss the sea. Even Brook can see it in your gaze when Aren comes back. And with what Iblon said today, you finally made your decision."

I sighed.

"He will understand," Koen said.

I sat up and looked at Koen with narrowed eyes. He didn't return my stare, his gaze still fixed on the sky above.

"There should be a rule against you knowing as much as you do about us."

Koen smirked. "So… When?"

"The Golden Eagle will be here for a week. When the crew has rested, I am off."

Koen nodded and sat up.

"Won't you ask about my role in the Brotherhood?"

He shrugged, "You had built your part of this with an easy way out. It doesn't matter if you are here on in the Red Sea, battling with men and women who want your skin."

"Others won't see it the same way."

"Iblon won't," Koen said with a nod. "Brook loves you, in the most selfless form I've ever seen. He will accept it and still consider you a part of the

Brotherhood."

"What about you?" I asked.

When he didn't answer, I sat up and looked at him again. This time Koen turned to me again and smiled.

"We were friends long before any of this had happened. You had come and gone so many times... I know you will always return," Koen sat up, his arm wrapped around my shoulders. "When we founded the Brotherhood, we only had to swear to something we already were. Brothers not in blood, but brothers, nevertheless."

I leaned on his shoulder. We sat there for a long time, not talking because we didn't have to say anything. The sky around us turned red and then orange. The bells of the temple rung, reverberating through our chest, calling for morning prayer.

The priest walked out in front of the gathering crowd, his staff clanking on the stones with each of his shuffling steps.

"Let's not ruin this night with the words of a useless man," Koen said.

He climbed to his feet and offered me his hand.

"One day you will have to tell me what's happened between the two of you."

"A man who keeps so many secrets can't reveal his own."

I shook my head and took his hand. Once on my feet, we clapped hands, and each of us went our own way.

I walked back into the Drunk Moon, and Brook followed me into the private room. The flowers and most of the candles were gone, the room as somber as it usually was.

"You are not the only visitor," Brook said when I looked at him with an arched brow. "I can't seem too tender to any of my clients and even less my enemies."

I took a seat on the couch, crossing my legs. Brook took a seat by my side, wrapping his arms around me.

"I won't be staying for much longer," I said after a long moment passed.

Brook took a deep breath but didn't answer.

"As soon as my crew has had their rest, I will be leaving with them for another contract with this magician you talked about. Helena, is it?"

Brook still didn't answer, his hand running up and down my arm.

"So, I guess," I said, turning my gaze towards him. "This thing between us… It's over."

"Only if you wish it so," Brook answered.

I lifted a brow, and Brook planted a kiss on it.

"What do you mean?" I asked when he didn't say a thing.

"You will come back, I presume… It might be in a month or in a turn, but you will be coming back."

"That's a given."

"Well, then… I told you this when we were much younger. I will be always waiting for you."

"That's not a normal relationship," I said.

"None of us fits into what others would define as normal. A priest would even say we are condemned."

"Not my type of priest."

"Exactly my point," Brook said.

"What do you propose?"

"Whatever you want, as long as we stay together. You want to spend five turns in the sea, and you see someone you like, go at it. And I pray to the Gods, yours and mine, it will never be longer than that."

"What about you?"

"My ego isn't that big so that I can't let the woman I love to be happy."

"So, you do love me? And here I thought my mercenary doesn't have a heart."

Brook laughed. "You got my heart the moment I saw you, and it's been yours ever since."

I nestled in the crook of his arm and battled the tears coming to my eyes.

"I love you, Brook."

"I know, iris."

We stayed locked in each other's arms until the morning broke. Then, Aren knocked on the door and walked into the private room.

"What is it?" I asked.

"We have to cut this stay short. The crew is getting restless. Ronald and Jim got into a brawl with a guard at the Singing Buccaneer today."

"What's the problem? Pay him up?"

"Out of luck. We stumbled on a guard too honest for his own good. His loyalty is with Donovan. He'll be on our heels soon."

I nodded and stood up.

"Before you leave..." Brook said catching my hand.

"I'll be on the Golden Eagle, gathering the crew," Aren said and walked out of the room.

I turned to Brook, and he had a big box in his hand.

"What's that?"

"Open it."

I lifted the top and took out a large red leather vest.

"Here, let me help you," Brook said, taking it out and holding it for me to put on. "When you are away, I want you to have something to remember me by, something that will keep you warm when I can't."

I smiled, a treacherous tear sliding down my cheek. Brook brushed it away and planted another kiss on my lips.

"Go before the Golden Eagle sails without you."

"Not a chance." I chuckled.

Stealing one last kiss, I dashed out of the Drunk Moon and across Query. A shadow followed me over the roofs of the city. I walked the gangplank to my ship, filling my lungs with the air full of salt. Turning my head to the sky, I let the sun kiss my skin, and a smile spread on my lips.

"Hey, boys. A cheer for the captain!" Aren cried.

Whistles and claps followed me to the captain's bridge. Heath stepped away, offering me my place in front of the wheel.

My crew stood in their mismatched clothes and weapons hanging at their belts.

"Well, sorry bunch of nitwits. What are you waiting for? The Red Sea awaits!" I cried.

***

Isabella walked to a window and looked at the endless sea.

"Brook is a smart man..."

"I had no doubt in that," the man said leaning back in his chair.

Isabella sighed and brushed the hair away from her face and tucked it under her bandanna. She turned around, walked to the chair, and picked her red leather vest.

"How long has it been since you two saw each other?" the man asked as Isabella walked to the door.

She slid her arms into the sleeves and turned to the man, her hand on the knob.

"Almost five turns."

ABOUT THE AUTHOR

Iren Adams is a new author who spends every moment of her time with books, reading them or writing them.

To learn more about Iren Adams, the new books to come and more information about the world of Yarrowind follow her on her social media:

Website: irenadams.ink

Twitter: @irenadamsblog

Facebook: @irenadamsblog

Pinterest: @irenadamsblog

The first instalment of *Chronicles of Yarrowind* as well as *Heroes of Yarrowind* are available on amazon.com.

EXCERPT FROM

CHRONICLES OF YARROWIND

THE AGE OF CHANGE

PROLOGUE

"How did you know this would happen?" the man asked.

"I do not have time to sit idly and answer your questions," the woman clad in white said.

"The Kings authorized this procedure. They want to know what happened."

The woman laughed, her eyes twinkling in the candlelight.

"And why do you think it matters to me what the so-called Kings do or want?"

"You promised to help," the man answered.

"I promised my help only to one being..."

"And that person asked you to do this."

"Fine... But you know the legends. You can guess how I knew."

The man fumbled with the pile of parchments

stacked on his desk.

"Is this a fair description of the events?" the man asked, sliding one of the parchments across the desk.

The woman took it in her hands and started to read.

***

The creature opened its eyes and looked around. For ages, it had enjoyed the dreamless sleep.

It wanted nothing more than to close its eyes and embrace the slumber.

But something must have happened to wake it up. It stood on all fours and shook its head.

The air was charged with energy. Dark energy. The strings of time and existence were thinning. The canvas of reality was in danger of being destroyed.

A loud roar escaped the creature's mouth. But no answer came. Its brothers and sisters were asleep. It was the first one to feel the change coming. The only one who could do anything about it.

But it had to be sure. The creature had to visit the place it left ages ago.

The view in front of it shifted and in tiny patches. The reality regrouped itself to form a new one, from another distant world.

The Halls of Obliteration stood untouched by the ages that had passed. But the place was no longer dead.

The energy pulsed through the ground, the walls, even the air itself. It came in waves from one of the statues sitting at the end of the hall.

Measuring each step, the creature walked to the statue of an ancient God. Dark energy was coming from the seated figure. All black and cloaked, its features hidden from view, the God was starting to awaken too.

"You will not be able to change my destiny!" a scream erupted in the creature's head.

It bowed its head and closed its eyes, a growl of anger and pain coming from its throat. The creature shook its head and turned to walk away, but a cloud of smoke appeared in the air. Shifting, a deformed face looked the creature in the eyes.

"You were such a wonderful pet once. And you will be again! That is if you don't want to die when my restraints shall fall," it whispered through clenched teeth. "You are still afraid of death... Are you not?"

"If you get what you so desire, there will be no way of stopping my death. I know that now. Your tricks once scared me... But not anymore! Someday you will perish, and I will be there to see it happen."

The smoke shifted, lips pursed, the face observed the creature.

"In that stupid head of yours, don't you see any possibility of my victory?!"

No answer came from the creature's lips. Not only one outcome led to the Dark God's victory... Thousands of possibilities, endless options, all rushing through its head. And they all led to the same thing. War, chaos, and destruction.

But something caught its omniscient eye. Blue

eyes and gray hair. A woman stood amidst the fire.

A croak, resembling a chuckle escaped the creature's lips.

A cry of a newborn baby came to its ears. A special being was born. A chance had been given to the creature. A tiny one but still a chance.

A cracking sound filled the hall. The creature bent its neck and twisted its body, its limbs shortening. And in a few moments, a woman clad in white stood watching in the dead eyes of the face of smoke.

"Farewell," she said, walking past the face that still waited for an answer. "Or better not."

A scream shook the walls and was the only answer. But the woman was already entering a portal she had opened.

She had to see the child. She had to know for sure she wasn't making a mistake. And if she was right, she had to make some preparations.

***

The woman put the parchment back on the table and pursed her lips.

"So, what do you think?" the man asked, leaning forward.

"Stories... Nothing more."

"Are you sure?"

"But so many stories are true..." the woman looked at the man with a smile that didn't quite reach her eyes.

"Was your premonition wrong?"

THE AGE OF CHANGE

"It is never wrong..."

PART I

The doom of the world is nigh.
The armies will march south again,
To reclaim what once was theirs.
All nations will stand united,
But rivers of blood will flow.
And the rise of the One will begin once more.
                Strokil of Kholtrem, *Prophecies Tome I*
                    Turn 685 of the First Age

CHAPTER 1

LOST

"It is an honor to meet you, Sir Borowick," the man said with a bow, indicating a chair for Borowick to occupy.

Borowick nodded his expression blank and took the seat.

"I have a lot of questions," the man said.

His finger slid over the parchment, his eyes following lines and lines of text.

"As long as you ask them quickly."

"I do not think this matter can be resolved quickly," the man said.

Borowick didn't answer.

"Right. Well... Let's start at the beginning, then."

Borowick's gaze didn't reveal a thing.

"How did you meet Lady Alanna?"

"Don't you know already?"

"I would rather hear it from you," the man said, his fingers playing with a feather quill.

"I don't see how this is useful to the Kings."

"Well... It is not for us to know. We are only here to obey orders."

"Right..."

"Will you tell me then?"

Borowick leaned back in the chair and put one of his gloved hands over the other.

***

There were four of us. Four young strong men, who knew there was nothing for us in Yago, a village full of fishers and farmers. No adventure, no coin, no nothing.

Ron had been nagging me to leave since forever. I had known him since we were boys when the enemy was the burden of the housework and not devouring hunger. Steven and Martin came into our group much later, but we trusted each other with our lives.

I had no father growing up and when my mother died, I had no one left to keep me in our old creaking house. When Ron asked again I didn't think twice and followed him out of Yago.

We would seek a post with the guards and if not we could be mercenaries. Trained in tavern fights and greedy for coin, we hoped for a rapid ascension in the capital of the Kingdom.

We faced a long trip and one devoid of danger. That is if you take the Highroads constructed by the late Queen Orelia. Paved roads and stone bridges crossing the Kingdom from any village to Sartron. In the plans. But we were far from the capital, and it was just stomped ground and creaking wooden bridges that swayed if too many men crossed it at once.

Nevertheless, it was safe. Patrols crossed it from time to time and the outlaws tended to stay away.

Half a day away from Haenna we were starving and tired. With little coin in our pockets, no warm beds or hot meals waited for us there and we decided to venture into the Dark Forest.

The stories about its dangers have existed since the first travelers wandered into it. But we were young and bold. Crossing the forest would be another tale we would tell around the fire. It would save us two days of the trip, and we could hunt a meal whenever hunger bothered us.

It took us five days to understand what a bad idea it was. The Darks Forest was home to elves, goblins, and powerful magic.

On the second day, we were going in circles. Four days in and no wild animal that we could kill, roast and eat, had crossed our path. Steven had found some wild berries, and after eating them he spent every possible break in the bushes. Any attempt at making a fire was useless. Only humid bark and branches covered the forest floor.

On the fifth day, the real trouble started. The goblins had found us. A big group. Twenty or so. Those evil creatures with dark gray skin, big black eyes, and ears that sit high atop their heads. They were small, but there were too many of them.

The goblins waited until the night fell to attack us. And they did it from behind our backs. One moment we were alone, the next one, a swarm of blows and kicks rained on us from every side.

It took us a moment, but we stroke back. Not that it helped us much. We had managed to kill only a couple of them when Ron got surrounded.

He was too far away. I had to get through five goblins that jumped on me from every side. My heavy sword, which I bought with all the coins I had saved, didn't help much. I didn't know it at the time, but a longsword is not the best weapon for close combat.

I killed one of them and wounded another. But then, a goblin jumped from behind and smashed a mace on Ron's head. Ron stumbled. He wanted to move his sword, but no strength was left in his body. He fell face-first and didn't move again.

Dead or not, there was no time to worry about him. Three of us were still standing. Slashes and gushes covered out bodies in different places. The dull weapons of the goblins found their way to our flesh.

Martin was keeping four of the creatures at bay, but Steven got surrounded by another five. A large, deep cut across his chest seeped blood through his shirt. His sword was slashing from side to side, but with each moment he moved slower.

I started towards him, but another group kept me at bay. I plunged my sword through the chest of one of the goblins and beheaded another. But there were so many of them that none of that mattered.

A goblin jumped from behind a tree and knocked Steven down. Long dirty fingers wrapped a bloody cleaver. It climbed on top of Steven's back, pulled his head up and slashed his throat with the rusty blade.

I cried in agony. We were not going to survive, but I would kill as many of them as possible.

Running towards dying Steven, I sent the goblin flying through the trees with the blade of my sword. His black blood spraying the rest of the group.

Kneeling to pick up Steven's short sword, pain burst through my temples.

I turned around, but my mind slipped away and I heard Kesareth's calling.

***

The man coughed and leaned back. Borowick didn't pay any attention to it. His eyes were fixed on his gloved hands. His fingers running over his ring finger.

"Does this have any relation to your encounter with Lady Alanna?"

"You asked me to tell what happened."

"I wondered if you could cut to the most important part."

"Either I tell the whole story, or I leave without adding anything else. It is up to you."

The man redressed himself and picked up the quill.

"Go on, then."

***

When I opened my eyes, I was all alone. Wet cold ground stretched under me.

I sat up, my head spinning. Bile rose to my lips. My fingers brushed the back of my head and found a dried crust of blood and hair.

The goblins had left and taken anything of use, leaving only my dead companions behind.

I struggled to my feet and limped to Ron's body. He still had a shirt on, and I didn't.

Watching over my shoulder, I took the shirt off. I could feel Kesareth's wrath. The Goddess who received the dead in her island was unhappy with my sacrilege. But I was more afraid of dying in the Dark Forest than bear a curse by the Goddess of Death.

I might be able to steal from my dead companions, but I couldn't leave them like that. I dragged them together, picking up a dagger that I found under Martin's body.

I didn't have much strength and the grave I dug with my hands and the knife covered half of their bodies. Dead leaves and fallen branches were the only thing I could do for them.

A silent prayer had left my lips before I pulled myself to my feet again.

A droplet felt on my face. Then another one. And then the rain downed on the forest. I left the unmarked grave when the forest was a wall of water and green.

I didn't walk for long the first day. My head kept spinning and I don't know how I didn't end up in the same place I started. But when I hid under a fallen tree, I could not move a muscle.

I woke up to the same forest, but full of mud and water. That's when I felt it. I guess it was there for a long time. But I hadn't noticed it before. Something was watching me.

I looked around and saw a wolf with white fur sitting on the ground. It was observing my every move.

I started running. I didn't know which way I needed to go, which way was the right way. I did know that I had to be as far away from that beast as possible when it decided it was hungry enough to attack me.

I didn't run for a long time. After no more than an hour it was more of a half walk and then I struggled to stand.

When I couldn't move my feet anymore, I used all the strength I had left to climb up the tree and fell asleep.

I woke up shaking. Cuts and bruises all over my body stung and hurt. But the cold was leaving my body senseless.

The wolf was sitting by the base of the tree and as soon as I woke up it trotted behind some bushes.

I climbed down and kept walking. From time to time the wolf would come closer, and I moved farther. Other times it wandered far behind the trees, and I felt the need to track it back down.

It might be hungry, but I was too. A hunter and a

hunted. Not sure who was who.

The sky split in two with rolling thunder and I don't know how it was possible, but the storm was worse than before. The wolf didn't seem to mind. Its fur stayed spotless and shiny.

There was a pattern in our pursuit. I would walk for as long as I could and then I would climb up a tree and try to sleep. The deafening thunder would not let me get the much-needed rest. When I felt unable to control my shaking body, I would climb down and keep walking. The wolf staying close day and night.

I didn't know how much time had passed. Day and night were one and the same. The heavy storm and thick branches didn't let any sunlight in.

My muscles were aching and I couldn't keep the cold away. Any longer and my teeth would shatter.

Putting one foot in front of the other, that was my only thought.

I remember falling but not much else. The next time I opened my eyes; the wolf was sitting at the edge of the clearing. Its eyes observing me, its fur shining.

The light blinded me. But when I managed to keep my eyes open, I found myself at the same spot. The rain had stopped, and the sun found its way through the deep foliage. Birds were chirping and the water trickled somewhere close.

A white stone lay on the grass next to me where the wolf sat a moment ago. I grabbed it in my hand, only because I couldn't resist the urge not to.

I had no strength left in my body, so I crawled to the edge of the water. There was a bush with berries, and I was halfway to it when I heard a voice.

"Don't move!"

I looked up and saw an arrow pointed at me. A group of elves sat nearby, one of them had seen me and had her bow ready.

"I..." I started, but my throat was full of rushing knives.

"Give me a reason to let the arrow find its mark," the woman added.

I put my hands up, but my battered mind had had enough. I fell into the river losing myself into the darkness.

***

The man didn't move when Borowick stopped talking.

Borowick stood up and went to fill a glass of water from a pitcher.

"Who was it?"

"Lady Alanna, of course."

"I know that. That's not what I mean."

Borowick's eyes twinkled in the candlelight.

"The wolf... Who was it?" the man insisted.

"I think you know."

"But it can't be."

"I found out she was always quite resourceful," Borowick said putting the glass down.

CHAPTER 2

PRISON OF HIS

Reese walked into the room and threw a rapid look around.

"Ah, Reese of Persla. Come," the man behind the desk said.

"How did your people find me?"

"I received help from the Kings... and the Chapter."

With a wince on his face, Reese walked to the chair.

"Will you tell me what happened?" the man asked taking the quill and a clean parchment.

"You already know everything. You've talked to everyone, before finding me."

"Not everyone. Not yet."

"Some people are harder to track than me?"

"Sadly, yes," the man said with a wince. "I have so

many questions. So many blanks to fill."

"Before we start, know this. If I would get the chance to go back and change anything, I would still do the same thing."

"There is no judgment. Only knowledge to be earned."

"We'll see about that," Reese said with a chuckle. "But I will tell you everything... Everything that happened."

***

Still a young member of the Academy I had found something that was supposed to be hidden. The Chapter caught up fast. There was nothing that could have helped me when they came for me. And I didn't even fight.

I should have. I should have cast any spell known to me. I should have broken their bodies. I should have run. Anything was better than what the Chapter had prepared for me.

One day, I was a respected magician, discovering new spells and ready to teach my first group of students. The next, I woke up in a soft bed that wasn't mine.

A spell of recognition left my lips, which would help me understand where I was. But when the first word left my mouth a burning pain tore through the skin on my neck. It drained me of my blood, my strength, and my consciousness.

When I opened my eyes, I was in the bed again,

under layers of thin blankets. My fingers brushed my neck, but the only thing they found was a thin bronze chain.

Getting out of bed, I cast another spell. But only a fool awaits a different result after doing the same thing. After a great amount of pain and dreamless sleep, I woke up in the bed again. Stranded in a castle that was my prison, I was left with no magic. Well, with no way to perform any spell. The burning of the chain saw to that.

I spent the first day wandering through the halls. There were a few rooms, but they stood bare. The doors that led outside, brought me to the withered inner garden.

In the dining hall, a large table stood. A dozen chairs and a meal prepared for one. The cold stew, the bitter wine, and the dry bread. The only thing I would get each and every day. No matter how hungry I was, no matter how early I reached the dining hall, a cold meal waited for me.

I did try to escape. But there was no way out. The only door that didn't lead to the garden was in the attic, and it allowed to access the roof.

I remember walking there for the first time. Endless sea surrounded the castle. Its waves crashed on the rocks in white foam, and my hopes died.

I sat there for hours, my gaze fixed on the horizon where the endless sea and the cloudless sky met and the lines blurred. I fell asleep there. Under the sky with no stars and with the wind that enveloped me in a warm embrace.

I woke up in my warm bed the next morning.

I searched for any way to escape, but the magic was more powerful than anything I knew. The constant throbbing of the burning skin reminded me of that.

Each time I touched the metal, my fingers burnt with an invisible fire. I cast a spell to heal myself, but even that made me wake up in the same bed again.

At first, I tried doing something with myself. But there was nothing to do. No book to read, no painting to observe. I even tried setting the garden, digging out the herbs with my bare hands, the ground coloring my nails black. But when I came back the next day, I would find everything in the same deplorable state as when I first saw it.

There were no mirrors, no glass to see if I was changing. If the time was consuming me. But nor my beard, nor my hair grew.

I was left with no possibility to cast a spell, in a desolate castle with no distraction, and forced to relive the same day over and over again. There was no sentence shorter than eternity when one went against the wishes of the Chapter.

I tried writing things that came to my mind. I would open my veins and use my blood to scribble on the walls. And later, I trained to do it with my magic. The pain in my neck tore me apart, but I forced myself to do it anyway.

But the next day my gaze would slide over the bare walls.

I knew I would lose my sanity. I couldn't even say

how much time had passed. Later, I figured out that was about half-way through my time in that place. Close to fifty turns. Fifty turns in an empty castle, with no other company but my thoughts.

I lived in fear of becoming one of the Lost. The magicians who dabbed in the dark forms of magic, losing their grip on reality.

The fear to see my mind slip like that... It gnawed on my mind. My thoughts turned dark.

I thought I had no other choice.

The only thing I wanted was peace, and I was ready to get it any way I could.

I didn't have many things available, so I knotted a few blankets and attached them to a wooden beam that held the ceiling.

The excitement that I felt... I can't describe it. I felt alive for the first time in a long time. Even though I hoped to die in a matter of minutes.

I remember smiling while my body twitched and the life slipped out of my body.

When I opened my eyes again, I cursed my luck. I was lying in the same bed, buried under the blankets.

I thought I made a mistake somewhere. I fell asleep or used my magic to keep me alive.

So, I tried again.

And again.

And again.

The next day, I jumped from the roof of the castle into the white and blue of the sea. But moments before my head would crush on the wet rocks, I would wake up in the same bed again.

I tried opening my veins, eating poisonous roots from the garden, drowning in my bath, accelerating my aging process. I even used the magic to send a powerful blast through my body, before the chain would drain me of my life.

But instead of dying I would wake up in the same bed, every time. There was no peace for my tormented soul.

I wandered through the halls of the castle, a shell devoid of purpose.

Some days, I didn't leave my bed. Other days I spent watching the unchanging horizon from the roof of my prison. And others I would get another idea on how to end it, I would try it, but I always ended in that bed again.

I don't know when it started... Which was the day that my mind started to slip away. But I saw shadows moving in the halls, my father's face dancing on the fire lashes. One day, it was a woman that appeared in the fire. A woman whom I once knew.

"Reese," she whispered. "We need you back."

I didn't move. I wouldn't help the madness take me. I would let it fight its way in, keeping my consciousness for as long as possible.

The face grew clearer, the features known to me, but long forgotten. Her black eyes burnt with fire, but I turned away.

"Reese, it is time..."

I closed my eyes, fighting the tears. Anything was better than this.

A warm hand caressed my face, and I gasped. The

world around me shifted and my head split with pain. The woman's face was still in front of mine, but I was no longer alone in the castle.

I brushed her away and looked around. The red brick walls of the Academy stood intact after a whole age I had spent in that prison.

I gasped, my lungs fighting for air. Each part of my body ached, my muscles stiff.

I looked around and saw hundreds of chairs, all but one occupied by magicians. They had a void look in their eyes as if they were not there. Prisoners of their minds.

Each of them had a chain of bronze around their necks. The smell of burning flesh came to my nose and I saw the same horrid scars I felt on my own neck.

Some of the magicians were young, no longer students but not masters yet. Others had the hair white as snow, their faces covered in wrinkles.

"Do you remember who you are?" the woman that woke me asked.

"Yes," I nodded, my throat dry and burning.

"Do you remember me?"

Her face was so familiar, but I couldn't place it. And then it came.

"Helena..."

"Yes, it is me," the woman said with a small smile on her lips. "I feared your mind might have slipped already, but it appears you are much stronger than we had presumed."

I didn't answer. This was wrong. I was not supposed to be back. The purpose was to let me go mad in that castle. And only then... Maybe then, I would be allowed to go back to the world.

I knew this would be my only chance and started to chant a spell. But fire ran through my neck and brought me to my knees. The chain was still in place, keeping my magic in check.

Helena clicked her tongue and walked to my side.

"Bad boy..." she whispered, lifting my chin with her long fingers.

She attached a pendant on my chain, and the pain became bearable.

"This will allow you to do some magic, but you will carry your prison with you. And know this... If you do anything... And when I say anything, I mean anything that would make me suspicious, you will end in the same place you were not an hour ago. Am I clear?"

I nodded, but I feared to lift my eyes to hers. The only thing that was real for me was the warmth of the metal against my skin.

"I have a mission for you," she said. Her hand caressed my face again, and her lips touched mine.

"Follow me," she said breaking the kiss.

I didn't wait to be told twice. I would do anything not to end up in the same prison I had been the last one hundred turns.

With one last gaze on all of those condemned to the same madness I have been, I followed Helena out of the hall.

***

"What were the charges?"

Reese chuckled, "Does it matter?"

The man nodded.

"Theft, attempted murder and... Treason."

The man scratched his forehead and added lines of text.

"Did anyone know?" the man asked.

"Me, Helena, the other three on the Chapter, of course..."

"No, I mean besides them."

"Helena might have told someone."

The man let out a sigh.

"Did you tell anyone? Anyone who could have helped?"

"No..."

"You didn't tell her?"

"No..." Reese said, his voice no louder than a whisper and shook his head. "She uncovered that one all by herself."

CHAPTER 3
NEWCOMMER

"Good morning, Lady Alanna," the man said standing up and bowing his head.

"Good morning... I am not sure I know your name."

"My name is not important. Only my job is."

The man guided Alanna to a chair and went back behind his desk.

"You look bothered," Alanna said.

"I assumed you wouldn't be alone."

"She had other business to attend to."

"I see," the man said with a nod, his gaze fixed on her but not catching her eye. "I had some questions for her."

"I am sure I can answer those for you."

The man shuffled in his seat.

"Is there something wrong?" Alanna asked.

"I didn't expect you to cooperate. None of the others were so forthcoming."

"Anything the Kings want..."

"It depends upon which of them is asking, I suppose."

"That is irrelevant," Alanna said, crossing her legs. After a minute she added. "Where do you want to start?"

"Let's start at the beginning."

***

My company was on a patrol of Anarem's borders. Goblins inhabit the southern part of the Dark Forest. King Inigo sends patrols there to let those dark creatures know that they are not welcome in Anarem.

We had stopped for a meal when a man covered in rags broke through the line of trees and knelt next to the river. I trained my bow on him, but he fainted at my feet.

Bruises and wounds covered each part of his skin that wasn't hidden by the ripped shirt and trousers. His skin was pale, draping his bones.

We had some healing herbs and potions, but nothing that could help a starved man. I didn't think he would survive the trip back to Anarem. But he did. Elian, my second in command, volunteered to carry him and Tarron couldn't avoid but to follow his example.

"Back so early, I see... Scared of your own

shadow, aren't you?" Morrigan said.

Leader of her own company, she was standing guard at the city's borders with them. She didn't like me much. Few did. But that was an argument for another time.

"We found a wounded man, starved to his bones. So either let me pass, or take him out of his misery yourself!" I snapped.

Morrigan looked over my shoulder and her eyes widened as she saw the man in Elian's and Tarron's arms. She moved to let us pass, and I sent Taenya to the healers to alert of our arrival.

King Inigo and the Advisers waited for us in the Healers' Hut. As soon as we laid him down, the healers started casting spells to keep him alive.

"You've left your post," the King said, his eyes boring into mine.

"Your Majesty," I said lowering my head, anger simmering under my skin. No action I did was ever good enough for him.

"Does it mean you cannot follow orders?"

"Am I supposed to let a man die?!"

The Advisers threw me looks as sharp as daggers, but I didn't care. The patrols were important, I knew that. But I would not leave a man in need of help to die.

"Why do you think the life of this man is more important than that of your fellow brothers and sisters? Don't you think the goblins will not use this opportunity to attack us?" the King asked.

"You, nor I, have the right to make this decision.

Life of a single man is no less important than that of all elves of Anarem. His life is worth saving. With or without a threat from the goblins."

"Do you doubt your King's orders?" Khator, one of the Advisers to the King asked.

"No blind follower is better than the one who follows with his heart," the King answered in my place. With a slight curve to his lips, he added, "You did well."

The King turned to leave, but one of the healers raised from his seat and approached him. He whispered something in his ear and showed him a white translucent stone. A wave of power washed over me and I blinked as the world swirled around me. Inigo's eyes were trained on me, worry drawing lines on his face.

"The Advisers will keep the stone, for now. Alanna, you will be his guard until he wakes up. Your company will keep with the training in the meantime," he said turning to leave. His white embroidered tunic floated behind him as well as his Advisers.

As soon as the stone disappeared with them, I could think with some clarity again. I was off the hook, but spending my time with the starved unconscious man wasn't something I was looking forward to.

"Elian, you know what to do," I said and Elian left the Healers' Hut. My second in command, he would lead the rest of the company back to the forest to continue the patrol.

The healers didn't wait to be alone to start slipping

potions in his mouth and covering his wounds with philters made from herbs.

Once he had a lean and muscular body. Now it was drained by hunger, carved by the fatigue and covered with cuts and bruises.

Twelve days had passed before he woke up. Confusion reigned on his face when he opened his eyes.

He attacked the healers. But even disarmed, with a weakened body, and facing trained elves he was a fearsome enemy. He broke an arm of one of them and almost strangled another.

When his eyes landed on me, he stopped. He put his arms in the air and allowed for the elves to tie him down.

For the next two weeks, I was his guard and his only company. His recovery was slow, and the Healers didn't let him out of the Hut.

He told me his name was Borowick, but he didn't say anything else. The only thing he asked was the stone. He wanted to have it back, even though he didn't know what it was. As soon as it was in his hands again, his composure calmed and he didn't make any more trouble. He waited for me. He waited for me to be ready to listen.

That suited me. I hated him for ruining my exercise. The patrols on the border were the last stages of my training. I wanted to be the leader of a company that if needed would part into battle.

But King Inigo had questions for him. How did he end up in the forest? How did he find the stone?

And how did he manage to survive in the forest for so long when he was alone?

I thought that the sooner he talked, the sooner he would depart from Anarem. That's why one evening when the healers left for the night I turned to him and asked, "What happened to you?"

Borowick looked at me with his pale green eyes but did not answer.

"Listen, they will keep you here until you tell everything. And let's be clear, all of us would be happier if you would be on your way."

His eyes bore into me, but no answer came from his lips. His fingers played with the stone, sending a wave of energy that rippled through me.

"What is this?"

"I don't know," Borowick finally answered.

"What do you mean?"

"I found it in the forest. Minutes before you found me."

I shook my head. Nothing about him made sense.

"I am telling you the truth," Borowick whispered.

"It may be. It may be..."

He told me about the small group he was a member of and how they got ambushed by the goblins. But the White Wolf was the only memory from the weeks he had spent in the forest alone.

After an hour he fell asleep, and I went to see King Inigo.

"Did you find something of interest?" he asked after the formal greeting, always straight to the matter at hand.

"Nothing much."

"Did he know what the stone was?"

"No..." I smirked. "Do you?"

"I might, but I am not sure. I need confirmation before I say anything..." the King said with a hard look in his eyes. "Did he tell you anything else?"

"Only that the White Wolf helped him to find his way. He thinks he didn't stumble on our company by a pure stroke of luck."

The King leaned forward in his seat, his half-braided gray hair sliding down his shoulders.

"White Wolf?" he asked.

"A hallucination I suppose... So starved as he was, he could have imagined anything."

"I very much doubt that. But that will be all for now. You can go. I don't want another wounded healer."

I sighed, he was brushing me away again... But he was my king, so I shook my head and said, "He wanted to know if he could stay after his wounds are healed."

"There will be no problem with him remaining in our city. As long as he decides to study our ways and adhere to them."

I nodded and left. The King and his Advisers deep in a discussion.

Another week passed before Borowick got out of the Healers' Huts. I was still his guard, even though he didn't need any. He was regaining his strength back.

He had told me he didn't have much training

before venturing into the Dark Forest. But his sheer strength could kill a lazy opponent.

Other elves started to like him. And I don't know how, but in a month, King Inigo allowed him to train for a captain. Borowick didn't have much free time, but any minute he got he would come to see me. With a flower in his hands.

Elian, Tarron, and Taenya loved to hang around when he was there. But Borowick sought to pass time with me alone.

I had finished my training and had free time to help him out and soon, even I enjoyed his company. We would spend every evening in the forest, talking about our culture. I don't know if it was of interest to him or he listened because he liked me.

Taenya joked about the moment Borowick would work up the courage to kiss me, and it made me blush every time.

I doubted it was true. No one in the Allied Kingdoms ever showed any interest in me. I was a daughter of an elf and a human, hated by both races. But my mother was late Queen Orelia, the Queen who united the humans under one ruler. And my father was late King Vanir, his son Inigo now sitting on the wooden throne in Anarem.

Even if hated, everyone respected me. But besides a few close friends, no one liked me.

Except Borowick as it seemed. And when he showed up with a flower in his hands and a stupid smile on his face, hidden under all the beard... I knew I wanted him to kiss me.

We spent the evening talking and laughing. When my friends left, Borowick put a hand around my waist. I turned my head with a smile on my lips.

His calloused fingers brushed my chin and pulled me closer to him. His lips touched mine and I couldn't think about anything else.

***

Alanna shifted and run her hand through her hair.

"I wasn't expecting that," the man said sitting back in his chair.

Alanna looked up at the man, but no words left her mouth.

"So much honesty."

"That's what you asked for."

"But you are the first one to give it to me," the man answered.

"I want to get to the bottom of this. As much as you do."

"Do you think that your relationship played a part in what has happened to him?"

"Maybe... Maybe not..." Alanna said, playing with an engraved ring on her finger. "Our relationship had an effect on many different things. But what happened to him... I doubt anyone could foresee that."

Printed in Great Britain
by Amazon